Praise for the novels of
New York Times and *USA TODAY*
bestselling author

DIANA PALMER

"Palmer demonstrates, yet again,
why she's the queen of desperado quests
for justice and true love."
—*Publishers Weekly* on *Dangerous*

"Nobody does it better."
—*New York Times* bestselling author Linda
Howard

"The popular Palmer has penned another
winning novel, a perfect blend of romance and
suspense."
—*Booklist* on *Lawman*

"Palmer knows how to make the sparks fly...
heartwarming."
—*Publishers Weekly* on *Renegade*

"Diana Palmer is a mesmerizing storyteller who
captures the essence of what a romance
should be."
—*Affaire de Coeur*

Also by Diana Palmer

Magnolia
Renegade
Lone Star Winter
Dangerous
Desperado
Heartless
Fearless
Her Kind of Hero
Nora
Big Sky Winter
Man of the Hour
Trilby
Lawman
Hard to Handle
Heart of Winter
Outsider
Night Fever
Before Sunrise
Noelle
Lawless

Diamond Spur
The Texas Ranger
Lord of the Desert
The Cowboy and the Lady
Most Wanted
Fit for a King
Paper Rose
Rage of Passion
Once in Paris
After the Music
Roomful of Roses
Champagne Girl
Passion Flower
Diamond Girl
Friends and Lovers
Cattleman's Choice
Lady Love
The Rawhide Man

Coming soon
The Savage Heart

DIANA PALMER

WYOMING TOUGH

DOUBLEDAY LARGE PRINT HOME LIBRARY EDITION

HQN™

This Large Print Edition, prepared especially for Doubleday Large Print Home Library, contains the complete, unabridged text of the original Publisher's Edition.

ISBN 978-1-61793-236-6

WYOMING TOUGH

This edition published by arrangement with Harlequin Books S.A.

® and TM are trademarks of the publisher. Trademarks indicated with ® are registered in the United States Patent and Trademark Office, the Canadian Trade Marks Office and in other countries.

Printed in U.S.A.

To my friend Kitty H.
with gratitude and much affection

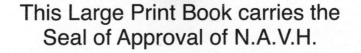

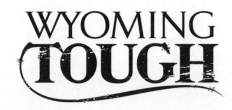

CHAPTER ONE

Edith Danielle Morena Brannt was not impressed with her new boss. The head honcho of the Rancho Real, or Royal Ranch in Spanish, near Catelow, Wyoming, was big and domineering and had a formidable bad attitude that he shared with all his hired hands.

Morie, as she was known to her friends, had a hard time holding back her fiery temper when Mallory Dawson Kirk raised his voice. He was impatient and hot-tempered and opinionated. Just like Morie's father, who'd opposed her decision to become a working cowgirl. Her dad opposed everything. She'd just told him she was going to find a job, packed her bags and left. She was twenty-three. He couldn't really stop her legally. Her mother, Shelby, had tried gentle reason. Her brother, Cort, had tried, too, with even less luck. She loved her family, but she was tired of being chased for who she was related to instead of who she was inside. Being a stranger on somebody else's property was an enchanting proposition. Even with Mallory's temper, she was happy being accepted for a poor, struggling female on her own in the harsh world. Besides that, she wanted to learn ranch work and her father refused to let her so much as lift a rope on his ranch. He didn't want her near his cattle.

"And another thing," Mallory said harshly, turning to Morie with a cold glare, "there's a place to hang keys when you're through with them. You never take a key out of the stable and leave it in your pocket. Is that clear?"

Morie, who'd actually transported the key to the main tack room off the property in her pocket at a time it was desperately needed, flushed. "Sorry, sir," she said stiffly. "Won't happen again."

"It won't if you expect to keep working here," he assured her.

"My fault," the foreman, old Darby Hanes, chimed in, smiling. "I forgot to tell her."

Mallory considered that and nodded finally. "That's what I always liked most about you, Darb, you're honest." He turned to Morie. "An example I'll expect you to follow, as our newest hire, by the way."

Her face reddened. "Sir, I've never taken anything that didn't belong to me."

He looked at her cheap clothes, the ragged hem of her jeans, her worn boots. But he didn't judge. He just nodded.

He had thick black hair, parted on one side and a little shaggy around the ears. He had big ears and a big nose, deep-set brown eyes under a jutting brow, thick eyebrows and a mouth so sensuous that Morie hadn't been able to take her eyes off it at first. That mouth made up for his lack of conventional good looks. He had big, well-manicured hands and a voice like deep velvet, as well as big feet, in old, rugged, dirt-caked boots. He was the boss, and nobody ever forgot it, but he got down in the mud and blood with his men and worked as if he was just an employee himself.

In fact, all three Kirk brothers were like that. Mallory was the oldest, at thirty-six. The second brother, Cane—a coincidence if there ever was one, considering Morie's mother's maiden name, even if hers was spelled with a *K*—was thirty-four, a veteran of the Second Gulf War, and he was missing an arm from being in the front lines in combat. He was confronting a drinking problem and undergoing therapy, which his brothers were trying to address.

The youngest brother, at thirty-one, was Dalton. He was a former border agent with the department of immigration, and his nickname was, for some odd reason, Tank. He'd been confronted by a gang of narco-smugglers on the Arizona border, all alone. He was shot to pieces and hospitalized for weeks, during which most of the physicians had given him up for dead because of the extent of his injuries. He confounded them all by living. Nevertheless, he quit the job and came home to the family ranch in Wyoming. He never spoke of the experience. But once Morie had seen him react to the backfire of an old ranch truck by diving to the ground. She'd laughed, but old Darby Hanes had silenced her and told her about Dalton's past as a border agent. She'd never laughed at his odd behaviors again. She supposed that both he and Cane had mental and emotional scars, as well as physical ones, from their past experiences. She'd never been shot at, or had anything happen to her. She'd been as sheltered as a hothouse orchid, both by her parents and her brother. This was her first taste of real life. She wasn't certain yet if she was going to like it.

She'd lived on her father's enormous ranch all her life. She could ride anything—her father had taught her himself. But she wasn't accustomed to the backbreaking work that daily ranch chores required, because she hadn't been permitted to do them at home, and she'd been slow her first couple of days.

Darby Hanes had taken her in hand and shown her how to manage the big bales of hay that the brothers still packed into the barn—refusing the more modern rolled bales as being in-efficient and wasteful—so that she didn't hurt herself when she lifted them. He'd taught her how to shoe horses, even though the ranch had a farrier, and how to doctor sick calves. In less than two weeks, she'd learned things that nothing in her college education had addressed.

"You've never done this work before," Darby accused, but he was smiling.

She grimaced. "No. But I needed a job, badly," she said, and it was almost the truth. "You've been great, Mr. Hanes. I owe you a lot for not giving me away. For teaching me what I needed to know here." And what a good thing it was, she thought privately, that her father didn't know. He'd have skinned Hanes alive for letting his sheltered little girl shoe a horse.

He waved a hand dismissively. "Not a problem. You make sure you wear those gloves," he added, nodding toward her back pocket. "You have beautiful hands. Like my wife used to," he added with a faraway look in his eyes and a faint smile. "She played the piano in a restaurant when I met her. We went on two dates and got married. Never had kids. She passed two years ago, from cancer." He stopped for a minute and took a long breath. "Still miss her," he added stiffly.

"I'm sorry," she said.

"I'll see her again," he replied. "Won't be too many years, either. It's part of the cycle, you see. Life and death. We all go through it. Nobody escapes."

That was true. How odd to be in a philosophical discussion on a ranch.

He lifted an eyebrow. "You think ranch hands are high-school dropouts, do you?" he mused. "I have a degree from MIT. I was their most promising student in theoretical physics, but my wife had a lung condition and they

wanted her to come west to a drier climate. Her dad had a ranch. . . ." He
stopped, chuckling. "Sorry. I tend to
run on. Anyway, I worked on the ranch
and preferred it to a lab. After she died,
I came here to work. So here I am. But
I'm not the only degreed geek around
here. We have three part-timers who
are going to college on scholarships
the Kirk brothers set up for them."

"What a nice bunch of guys!" she exclaimed.

"They really are. All of them seem
tough as nails, and they mostly are, but
they'll help anyone in need." He shifted.
"Paid my wife's hospital bill after the insurance lapsed. A small fortune, and
they didn't even blink."

Her throat got tight. What a gener-
ous thing to do. Her family had done
the same for people, but she didn't
dare mention that. "That was good of
them," she said with genuine feeling.

"Yes. I'll work here until I die, if they'll
keep me. They're great people."

They heard a noise and turned
around. The boss was standing behind
them.

"Thanks for the testimonial, but I believe there are cattle waiting to be dipped in the south pasture. . . ." Mallory commented with pursed lips and twinkling dark eyes.

Darby chuckled. "Yes, there are. Sorry, boss, I was just lauding you to the young lady. She was surprised to find out that I studied philosophy."

"Not to mention theoretical physics," the boss added drily.

"Yes, well, I won't mention your degree in biochemistry if you like," Darby said outrageously.

Mallory quirked an eyebrow. "Thanks."

Darby winked at Morie and left them alone.

Mallory towered over the slight brunette. "Your name is unusual. Morie . . . ?"

She laughed. "My full name is Edith Danielle Morena Brannt," she replied. "My mother knew I'd be a brunette, because both my parents are, so they added *morena,* which means *brunette* in Spanish. I had, uh, Spanish great-grandparents," she stuttered, having almost given away the fact that they were titled Spanish royalty. That would never do. She wanted to be perceived as a poor, but honest, cowgirl. Her last name wasn't uncommon in South Texas, and Mallory wasn't likely to connect it with King Brannt, who was a true cattle baron.

He cocked his head. "Morie," he said. "Nice."

"I'm really sorry, about the key," she said.

He shrugged. "I did the same thing last month, but I'm the boss," he added firmly. "I don't make mistakes. You remember that."

She gave him an open smile. "Yes, sir."

He studied her curiously. She was small and nicely rounded, with black hair that was obviously long and pulled into a bun atop her head. She wasn't beautiful, but she was pleasant to look at, with those big brown eyes and that pretty mouth and perfect skin. She didn't seem the sort to do physical labor on a ranch.

"Sir?" she asked, uncomfortable from the scrutiny.

"Sorry. I was just thinking that you don't look like the usual sort we hire for ranch hands."

"I do have a college degree," she defended herself.

"You do? What was your major?"

"History," she said, and looked defensive. "Yes, it's dates. Yes, it's about the past. Yes, some of it can be boring. But I love it."

He looked at her thoughtfully. "You should talk to Cane. His degree is in anthropology. Pity it wasn't paleontology, because we're close to Fossil Lake. That's part of the Green River Formation, and there are all sorts of fossils there. Cane loved to dig." His face hardened. "He won't talk about going back to it."

"Because of his arm?" she asked bluntly. "That wouldn't stop him. He could do administrative work on a dig." She flushed. "I minored in anthropology," she confessed.

He burst out laughing. "No wonder you like ranch work. Did you go on digs?" He knew, as some people didn't, that archaeology was one of four sub-fields of anthropology.

"I did. Drove my mother mad. My clothes were always full of mud and I looked like a street child most of the time." She didn't dare tell him that she'd come to dinner in her dig clothing when a famous visiting politician from Europe was at the table, along with some members of a royal family. Her father had been eloquent. "There were some incidents when I came home muddy," she added with a chuckle.

"I can imagine." He sighed. "Cane hasn't adjusted to the physical changes. He's stopped going to therapy and he won't join in any family outings. He stays in his room playing online video games." He stopped. "Good Lord, I can't believe I'm telling you these things."

"I'm as quiet as a clam," she pointed out. "I never tell anything I know."

"You're a good listener. Most people aren't."

She smiled. "You are."

He chuckled. "I'm the boss. I have to listen to people."

"Good point."

"I'll just finish getting those bales of hay stacked," she said. She stopped and glanced up at him. "You know, most ranchers these days use the big bales. . . ."

"Stop right there," he said curtly. "I don't like a lot of the so-called improvements. I run this ranch the way my dad did, and his dad before him. We rotate crops, and cattle, avoid unnecessary supplements, and maintain organic crops and grass strains. And we don't allow oil extraction anywhere on this ranch. Lots of fracking farther south in Wyoming to extract oil from shale deposits, but we won't sell land for that, or lease it."

She knew they were environmentally sensitive. The family had been featured in a small northwestern cattlemen's newspaper that she'd seen lying on a table in the bunkhouse.

"What's fracking?" she asked curiously.

"They inject liquids at high speed into shale rock to fracture it and allow access to oil and gas deposits. It can contaminate the water table if it isn't done right, and some people say it causes earthquakes." His dark eyes were serious. "I'm not taking any chances with our water. It's precious."

"Yes, sir," she replied.

He shrugged. "No offense. I've had the lectures on the joys of using genetically modified crops and cloning." He leaned down. "Over my dead body."

She laughed in spite of herself. Her elfin face radiated joy. Her dark eyes twinkled with it. He looked at her for a long moment, smiling quizzically. She was pretty. Not only pretty, she had a sense of humor. She was unlike his current girlfriend, a suave eastern sophisticate named Gelly Bruner, whose family had moved to Wyoming a few years previously and bought a small ranch near the Kirks. They met at a cocktail party in Denver, where her father was a speaker at a conference Mallory had attended. He and Gelly went around together, but he had no real interest in a passionate relationship. Not at the moment anyway. He'd had a bad experience in the past that had soured him on relationships. He knew instinctively that Gelly would only be around as long as he had money to spend on her. He had no illusions about his lack of good looks. He got women because he was rich. Period.

"Deep thoughts, sir?" she teased.

He laughed curtly. "Too deep to share. Get to work, kid. If you need anything, Darby's nearby."

"Yes, sir," she replied, and wondered for a moment if she was somehow in the military. It seemed right to give him that form of address. She'd heard cowboys use it with her father since she was a child. Some men radiated authority and resolve. Her father was one. So was this man.

"Now you're doing the deep-thinking thing," he challenged.

She laughed. "Just stray thoughts. Nothing interesting."

His dark eyes narrowed. "What was your favorite period? In history," he added.

"Oh! Well, actually, it was the Tudor period."

Both thick, dark eyebrows went up.

"Really. And which Tudor was your favorite?"

"Mary."

His eyebrows levered up a fraction. "Bloody Mary?"

She glared at him. "All the Tudor monarchs burned people. Is it less offensive to burn just a few rather than a few hundred? Elizabeth burned people, and so did her father and her brother. They were all tarred with the same brush, but Elizabeth lived longer and had better PR than the rest of her family."

He burst out laughing.

"Well, it's true," she persisted. "She was elevated to mystic status by her supporters."

"Indeed she was." He grimaced. "I hated history."

"Shame."

He laughed again. "I suppose so. I'll have to read up on the Tudors so that we can have discussions about their virtues and flaws."

"I'd enjoy that. I like debate."

"So do I, as long as I win."

She gave him a wicked grin and turned back to her work.

The bunkhouse was quiet at night. She had a small room of her own, which was maintained for female hires. It was rough and sparsely accommodated, but she loved it. She'd brought her iPad along, and she surfed the internet on the ranch's wireless network and watched films and television shows on it. She also read a lot. She hadn't been joking about her passion for history. She still indulged it, out of college, by seeking out transcripts of Spanish manuscripts that pertained to Mary Tudor and her five-year reign in England. She found the writings in all sorts of odd places. It was fascinating to her to walk around virtual libraries and sample the history that had been painstakingly translated into digital images. What a dedicated group librarians must be, she marveled, to offer so much knowledge to the public at such a cost of time and skill. And what incredible scholarship that gave someone the skills to read Latin and Greek and translate it into modern English, for the benefit of historians who couldn't read the ancient languages.

She marveled at the tech that was so new and so powerful. She fell asleep imagining what the future of electronics might hold. It was entrancing.

Just at dawn, her cell phone rang. She answered it in a sleepy tone.

"Sleepyhead" came a soft, teasing voice.

She rolled over onto her back and smiled. "Hi, Mom. How's it going at home?"

"I miss you," Shelby said with a sigh. "Your father is so bad-tempered that even the old hands are hiding from him. He wants to know where you are."

"Don't you dare tell him," Morie replied.

She sighed again. "I won't. But he's threatening to hire a private detective to sniff you out." She laughed. "He can't believe his little girl went off to work for wages."

"He's just mad that he hasn't got me to advise him on his breeding program and work out the kinks in his spreadsheets." She laughed. "I'll come home soon enough."

"In time for the production sale, I hope," Shelby added. The event was three weeks down the road, but King Brannt had already made arrangements for a gala event on the ranch during the showing of his prize Santa Gertrudis cattle on Skylance, the family ranch near San Antonio. It would be a party of epic proportions, with a guest list that included famous entertainers, sports figures, politicians and even royalty, and he'd want his whole family there. Especially Morie, who was essential to the hostessing. It would be too much for Shelby alone.

"I'll come back even if it's just for the night," Morie promised. "Tell Dad, so he doesn't self-destruct." She laughed.

"I'll tell him. You're like him, you know," she added.

"Cort's a lot more like him. What a temper!"

"Cort will calm right down when he finally finds a woman who can put up with him."

"Well, Dad found you," Morie noted. "So there's hope for Cort."

"You think so? He won't even go on dates anymore after that entertainment rep tried to seduce him in a movie theater. He was shocked to the back teeth when she said she'd done it in all sorts of fancy theaters back home." She laughed. "Your brother doesn't live in the real world. He thinks women are delicate treasures that need nourishing and protecting." She paused for a moment, then continued. "He really needs to stop watching old movies."

"Have him watch some old Bette Davis movies," Morie advised. "She's the most modern actress I ever saw, for all that her heyday was in the 1940s!"

"I loved those movies," Shelby said.

"Me, too." Morie hesitated. "I like Grandma's old movies."

Maria Kane had been a famous movie star, but she and Shelby had never been close and theirs had been a turbulent and sad relationship. It was still a painful topic for Shelby.

"I like them, too," Shelby said, surprisingly. "I never really knew my mother.

I was farmed out to housekeepers at first and then to my aunt. My mother never grew up," she added, remembering something Maria's last husband, Brad, had said during the funeral preparations in Hollywood.

Morie heard that sad note in her mother's voice and changed the subject. "I miss your baked fish."

Shelby laughed. "What a thing to say."

"Well, nobody makes it like you do, Mom. And they're not keen on fish around here, so we don't have it much. I dream of cod fillets, gently baked with fresh herbs and fresh butter . . . Darn, I have to stop drooling on my pillow!"

"When you come home, I'll make you some. You really need to learn to make them yourself. If you do move out and live apart from us, you have to be able to cook."

"I can always order out."

"Yes, but fresh food is so much nicer."

"Yours certainly is." She glanced at her watch. "Got to go, Mom. We're dipping cattle today. Nasty business."

"You should know. You were always in the thick of it here during the spring."

"I miss you."

"I miss you, too, sweetheart."

"Love you."

"Love you, too. Bye."

She hung up, then got out of bed and dressed. Her mother was one in a million, beautiful and talented, but equally able to whip up exotic meals or hostess a dinner party for royalty. Morie admired her tremendously.

She admired her dad, too, but she was heartily sick of men who took her out only with one end in mind—a marriage that would secure their financial futures. It was surprising how many of them saw her as a ticket to independent wealth. The last one had been disconcertingly frank about how his father advised him to marry an heiress, and that Morie was at least more pleasant to look at than some of the other rich men's daughters he'd escorted.

She was cursing him in three languages when her father came in, listened to her accusations and promptly escorted the young man off the property.

Morie had been crushed. She'd really liked the young man, an accountant named Bart Harrison, who'd come to town to audit a local business for his firm. It hadn't occurred to her at first that he'd searched her out deliberately at a local fiesta. He'd known who she was and who her family was, and he'd pursued her coldly, but with exquisite manners, made her feel beautiful, made her hungry for the small attentions he gave with such flair.

She'd been very attracted to him. But when he started talking about money, she backed away and ran. She wanted something more than to be the daughter of one of the richest Texas ranchers. She wanted a man who loved her for who she really was.

Now, helping to work cattle through the smelliest, nastiest pool of dip that she'd ever experienced in her life, she wondered if she'd gone mad to come here. May had arrived. Calving was in full swing, and so was the dipping process necessary to keep cattle pest-free.

"It smells like some of that fancy perfume, don't it?" Red Davis asked with a chuckle. He was in his late thirties, with red hair and freckles, blue eyes and a mischievous personality. He'd worked ranches most of his life, but he never stayed in one place too long. Morie vaguely remembered hearing her father say that Red had worked for a former mercenary named Cord Romero up near Houston.

She gave him a speaking look. "I'll never get the smell out of my clothes," she wailed.

"Why, sure you can," the lean, red-headed cowboy assured her, grinning in the shade of his wide-brimmed straw hat. "Here's what you do, Miss Morie. You go out in the woods late at night and wait till you see a skunk. Then you go jump at him. That's when he'll start stamping his front paws to warn you before he turns around and lifts his tail. . . ."

"Red!" she groaned.

"Wait, wait, listen," he said earnestly.

"After he sprays you and you have to bury your clothes and bathe in tomato juice, you'll forget all about how this old dipping-pool smells. See? It would solve your problem!"

"I'll show you a problem," she threatened.

He laughed. "You have to have a sense of humor to work around cattle," he told her.

"I totally agree, but there is nothing at all funny about a pond full of . . . Aaahhhhh!"

As she spoke, a calf bumped into her and knocked her over. She landed on her breasts in the pool of dip, getting it in her mouth and her eyes and her hair. She got to her knees and brought her hands down on the surface of the liquid in an eloquent display of furious anger. Which only made the situation worse, and gave Red the opportunity to display his sense of humor to its true depth.

"Will you stop laughing?" she wailed.

"Good God, are we dipping people now?" Mallory wanted to know.

Morie didn't think about what she

was doing; she was too mad. She hit the liquid with her hand and sent a spray of it right at Mallory. It landed on his spotless white shirt and splattered up into his face.

She sat frozen as she realized what she'd just done. She'd thrown pest dip on her boss. He'd fire her for sure. She was now history. She'd have to go home in disgrace . . . !

Mallory wiped his face with a hand-kerchief and gave her a long, speaking look. "Now that's why I never wear white shirts around this place," he commented with a dry look at Red, who was still doubled over laughing. "God knows what Mavie will say when she has to deal with this, and it's your fault," he added, pointing his finger at Morie. "You can explain it to her while you duck plates, bowls, knives or whatever else she can get to hand to throw at you!"

Mavie was the housekeeper and she had a red temper. Everybody was terrified of her.

"You aren't going to fire me?" Morie asked with unusual timidity.

He pursed his sensuous lips and his dark eyes twinkled. "Not a lot of modern people want to run cattle through foul-smelling pest-control substances," he mused. "It's easier to take a bath than to find somebody to replace you."

She swallowed hard. The awful-smelling stuff was in her nostrils. She wiped at it with the handkerchief. "At least I won't attract mosquitoes now." She sighed.

"Want to bet?" Red asked. "They love this stuff! If you rub it on your arms, they'll attack you in droves. . . . Where are you going, boss?"

Mallory just chuckled as he walked away. He didn't even answer Red.

Morie let out a sigh of relief as she wiped harder at her face. She shook her head and gave Red a rueful wince. "Well, that was a surprise," she murmured drily. "Thought I was going to be an ex-employee for sure."

"Naw," Red replied. "The boss is a good sport. Cane got into it with him one time over a woman who kept calling and harassing him. Boss put her through, just for fun. Cane tossed him headfirst into one of the watering troughs."

She laughed with surprise. "Good grief!"

"Shocked the boss. It was the first time Cane did anything really physical since he got out of the military. He thinks having one arm slows him down, limits him. But he's already adjusting to it. The boss ain't no lightweight," he added. "Cane picked him up over one shoulder and threw him."

"Wow."

He sobered. "You know, they've all got problems of one sort or another. But they're decent, honest, hardworking men. We'd do anything for them. They take care of us, and they're not judgmental." Red grimaced at some bad memory. "If they were, I'd sure be out on my ear."

"Slipped up, did you?" She gave him a quizzical look. "You, uh, didn't throw pesticide on the boss?"

He shook his head. "Something much worse, I'm afraid. All I got was a little jail time and a lecture from the boss."

He smiled. "Closest call I've had in re-cent years."

"Most people mess up once in a while," she said kindly.

"That's true. The only thing that will get you fired here is stealing," he added. "I don't know why it's such an issue with the boss, but he let a guy go last year for taking an expensive drill that didn't belong to him. He said he wouldn't abide a thief on the place. Cane, now, almost jumped the guy." He shook his head. "Odd, odd people in some re-spects."

"I suppose there's something that happened to them in the past," she conjectured.

"Could be." He made a face. "That girl, Gelly, that the boss goes around with has a shifty look," he added in a lowered tone. "There was some talk about her when she and her dad first moved here, about how they got the old Barnes property they're living on." He grimaced. "She's a looker, I'll give her that, but I think the boss is out of his noggin for letting her hang around.

Funny thing about that drill going missing," he added with narrowed, thoughtful eyes. "She didn't like the cowboy because he mouthed off to her. She was in the bunkhouse just before the boss found the missing drill in the guy's satchel, and the cowboy cussed a blue streak about being innocent. It didn't do any good. He was let go on the spot."

She felt cold chills down her spine. She'd only seen the boss's current love interest once, and it had been quite enough to convince her that the woman was putting on airs and pretending a sophistication she didn't really have. Most men weren't up on current fashions in high social circles, but Morie was, and she knew at first glance that Gelly Bruner was wearing last year's colors and fads. Morie had been to Fashion Week and subscribed, at home, to several magazines featuring the best in couture, both in English and French. Her wardrobe reflected the newer innovations. Her mother, Shelby, had been a top model in her younger days, and she knew many famous designers who were happy to outfit her daughter.

She didn't dare mention her fashion sense here, of course. It would take away her one chance to live like a normal, young single woman.

"You went to college recently, didn't you?" Red asked. He grinned at her surprise. "There's no secrets on a ranch. It's like a big family . . . we know everything."

"Yes, I did," she agreed, not taking offense.

"You live in them coed dorms, with men and women living together?" he asked, and seemed interested in her answer.

"No, I didn't," she said curtly. "My parents raised me very strictly. I guess I have old attitudes because of it, but I wasn't living in a dorm with single men." She shrugged. "I lived off campus with a girlfriend."

He raised both eyebrows. "Well, aren't you a dinosaur!" he exclaimed, but with twinkling eyes and obvious approval.

"That's right—I should live in a zoo." She made a wry face. "I don't fit in with modern society. That's why I'm out here," she added.

He nodded. "That's why most of us are out here. We're insulated from what people call civilization." He leaned down. "I love it here."

"So do I, Red," she agreed.

He glanced at the cattle and grimaced. "We'd better get this finished," he said, looking up at the sky. "They're predicting rain again. On top of all that snowmelt, we'll be lucky if we don't get some more bad flooding this year."

"Or more snow," she said, tongue-in-cheek. Wyoming weather was unpredictable; she'd already learned that. Some of the local ranchers had been forced to live in town when the snow piled up so that they couldn't even get to the cattle. Government agencies had come in to airlift food to starving animals.

Now the snowmelt was a problem. But so were mosquitoes in the unnaturally warm weather. People didn't think mosquitoes lived in places like Wyoming and Montana, but they thrived everywhere, it seemed. Along with other pests that could damage the health of cattle.

"You come from down south of here, don't you?" Red asked. "Where?"

She pursed her lips. "One of the other states," she said. "I'm not telling which one."

"Texas."

Her eyebrows shot up. He laughed. "Boss had a copy of your driver's license for the files. I just happened to notice it when I hacked into his personnel files."

"Red!"

"Hey, at least I stopped hacking CIA files," he protested. "And darn, I was enjoying that until they caught me."

She was shocked.

He shrugged. "Most men have a hobby of some sort. At least they didn't keep me locked up for long. Even offered me a job in their cybercrime unit." He laughed. "I may take them up on it one day. But for now, I'm happy being a ranch hand."

"You are full of surprises," she exclaimed.

"You ain't seen nothing yet," he teased. "Let's get back to work."

CHAPTER TWO

The small town near the ranch was called Catelow, named after a settler who came out west for his health in the early 1800s. He and his family, and some friends who were merchants, petitioned for and got a railhead established so that he could ship cattle east from his ranch property. A few of his descendants still lived locally, but more and more of the younger citizens went out of state to big cities for high-tech jobs that paid better wages.

Still, the town had all the necessary amenities. Catelow had a good police force, a fire department, a shopping mall, numerous ethnic restaurants, a scattering of Protestant churches and a Catholic one, a city manager from California who was a whiz at making a sickly city government thrive, and a big feed store next to an even bigger hardware store.

There was also a tractor dealership. From her childhood, following her father around various vendors, she'd been fascinated with heavy machinery. Once, while she was in college, for her birthday present King Brannt had actually rented a Caterpillar earthmover and had the driver teach her how to operate it. She'd had her brother, Cort, do home movies of the event. The rat wouldn't edit out the part where she drove the machine into a ditch and got it stuck in the mud, however. Cort had a wicked sense of humor, like King's younger brother, Danny, who was now a superior court judge, happily married to his former secretary, redheaded Edie Jackson. They had two sons.

She walked down the rows of tractors, sighing over a big green one that could probably have done everything short of cook a meal. It even had a cab to keep the sun off the driver.

"This is how you spend your day off, looking at tractors?" a sarcastic feminine voice asked from behind her.

Startled, she turned to find Mallory with Gelly Bruner clinging to his arm.

"I like tractors," Morie said simply. She glared at the other woman, whose obviously tinted blond hair was worn loose, with gem clips holding it back. She was dressed in a clinging silk dress with high, spiky heels and a sweater. It was barely May, and some days were still chilly. "Something wrong with that?"

"It's not very womanly, is it?" Gelly sighed. She shifted in a deliberate way that emphasized her slender curves. She moved closer to Mallory and beamed up at him. "I'd much rather browse in a Victoria's Secret shop," she purred.

"Oh, yes, I can certainly see myself dipping cattle wearing one of those camisole sets," Morie replied with a rueful grin.

"I can't see you wearing anything . . . feminine, myself," Gelly returned. Her smile had an ugly edge to it. "You aren't really a girlie girl, are you?"

Morie, remembering how she'd turned heads in a particularly exquisite oyster-colored gown from a famous French designer, only stared at Gelly without speaking. The look was unanswerable, and it made the other woman furious.

"I hate tractors, and it's chilly out here," Gelly told Mallory, tugging at his arm. "Can't we get a cappuccino in that new shop next to the florist?"

Mallory shrugged. "Suits me." He glanced at Morie. "Want to come?" he asked.

Morie was shocked and pleased by the request. The boss, taking the hired help out for coffee? She pondered doing it, just to make the other woman even madder. Gelly was flushed with anger by now.

"Thanks," she said. "But I'm having fun looking at the equipment."

Gelly relaxed and Mallory seemed perplexed.

"I'm buying," he added.

Which indicated that he thought Morie couldn't afford the expensive coffee and was declining for that reason. She felt vaguely offended. Of course, he knew nothing about her background. Her last name might be unusual, but she'd seen it in other states, even in other countries. He wasn't likely to connect a poor working girl with a famous cattleman, even if he might have met her father at some point. He ran Santa Gertrudis cattle, and her father's Santa Gertrudis seed bulls were famous, and much sought after at very high prices, for their bloodlines.

She cleared her throat. "Yes, well, thanks, but not today."

Mallory smiled oddly. "Okay. Have fun."

"Thanks."

They moved away, but not quickly enough for her to miss Gelly's muttered, "Very egalitarian of you to offer cappuccino to the hired help," she said in a tone that stung. "I bet she doesn't even know what it is."

Morie gritted her teeth. *One day, lady,* she thought, *you're going to get yours.*

She turned back to the tractors with a sigh.

A red, older-model sports car roared up at the office building and stopped in a near skid. The door opened and closed. A minute later, a pleasant tall man with light brown hair and dark eyes came up to her. He was wearing a suit, unusual in a rural town, except for bankers.

He glanced at her with a smile. "Looking to buy something?"

"Me? Oh, no, I work on a ranch. I just like heavy equipment."

His eyebrows arched. "You do?"

She laughed. "I guess it sounds odd."

"Not really," he replied. "My mom always said she married my dad because he surrounded himself with backhoes and earthmovers. She likes to drive them."

"Really!"

"My dad owns this." He waved his

hand at the tractors. "I'm sales and marketing," he added with a grimace. "I'd rather work in advertising, but Dad doesn't have anybody else. I'm an only child."

"Still, it's not a bad job, is it?" she asked pleasantly.

He chuckled. "Not bad at all, on some days." He extended a well-manicured hand. "Clark Edmondson," he introduced himself.

She shook it. "Morie Brannt."

"Very nice to meet you, Miss . . . Ms. . . . Mrs. . . . ?" he fished.

"Ms.," she said, laughing. "But I'm single."

"What a coincidence. So am I!"

"Imagine that."

"Are you really just looking, or scouting out a good deal for your boss?"

"I'm sure my boss can do his own deals," she replied. "I work for Mallory Kirk at the Rancho Real," she added.

"Oh. Him." He didn't look impressed.

"You know him."

"I know him, all right. We've had words a time or two on equipment repairs. He used to buy from us. Now he buys from a dealer in Casper." He shrugged. "Well, that's old news. A lot of locals work for him, and he doesn't have a large turnover. So I guess he's good to his employees even if he's a pain in the neck to vendors."

She laughed. "I suppose."

He cocked his head and looked down at her with both hands in his pockets. "You date?"

She laughed, surprised. "Well, sort of. I mean, I haven't recently."

"Like movies?"

"What sort?"

"Horror," he said.

"I like the vampire trilogy that's been popular."

He made a face.

"I like all the new cartoon movies, the Harry Potter ones, the Narnia films and anything to do with *Star Trek* or *Star Wars*," she told him.

"Well!"

"How about you?"

"I'm not keen on science fiction, but I haven't seen that new werewolf movie." He pursed his lips. "Want to go see it with me? There's a community theater.

It doesn't have a lot of the stuff the big complexes do, but it's not bad. There's a Chinese restaurant right next door that stays open late."

She hesitated. She wasn't sure this was a good idea. He looked like a nice man. But her new boss seemed to be a fair judge of character and he wouldn't do business here. It was a red flag.

"I'm mostly harmless," he replied. "I have good teeth, I only swear when really provoked, I wear size-eleven shoes and I've only had five speeding tickets. Oh, and I can speak Norwegian."

She stared at him, speechless. "I've never known anyone who could speak Norwegian."

"It will come in handy if I ever go to Norway," he replied with a chuckle. "God knows why I studied it. Spanish or French or even German would have made more sense."

"I think you should learn what you want to learn."

"So. How about the movie?"

She glanced at her watch. "I have to

help with calving, so I'm mostly on call for the rest of the weekend. It's already past time I was back at work. I only have a half day on Saturdays."

"Darn. Well, how about next Friday night? If calving permits?"

"I'll ask the boss," she said.

He raised an eyebrow.

"I have to," she replied. "I'm a new hire. I don't want to risk losing my job for being AWOL."

"Sounds like the military," he suggested.

"I guess so. It sort of feels like it, on the ranch, too."

"All three of the brothers fought overseas," he said. "Two of them didn't fare so well. Mallory, though, he's hard to dent."

"I noticed." She hadn't known that Mallory had been in the military, but it made sense, considering his air of authority. He was probably an officer, as well, when he'd been on active duty.

She saw him staring, waiting. She grimaced. "If I can get the time off, I'd like to see the film."

He beamed. "Great!"

She sighed. "I've forgotten how to go on a date. I'll have to go in jeans and a shirt. I didn't bring a dress or even a skirt to the ranch when I hired on. All my stuff is back home with my folks."

"You're noticing the suit. I wear it to impress potential customers," he said with a grin. "Around town, I mostly wear slacks and sport shirts, so jeans will be fine. We aren't exactly going to a ball, Cinderella," he added with twinkling eyes. "And I'm no prince."

"I think they're rewriting that fairy tale so that Cinderella is CEO of a corporation and she rescues a poor dockworker from his evil stepbrothers," she said, tongue-in-cheek.

"God forbid!" he exclaimed. "Don't women want to be women anymore?"

"Apparently not, if you watch television or films much." She sighed. She looked down at her own clothing. "Modern life requires us to work for a living, and there are only so many jobs available. Not much economically viable stuff for girls who lounge around in eye-

let and lace and drink tea in parlors."
Her dark eyes smiled.

"Did I sound sarcastic? I didn't mean
to. I like feminine women, but I think
lady wrestlers are exciting when they
do it in mud."

She laughed explosively. "Sexist!"

"Hey, I'd watch two men wrestle in
mud, too. I like mud."

She remembered being covered in
that, and pesticide, on the ranch and
winced. "You wouldn't if you had to
dip cattle around it," she promised
him.

"Good thing I don't know anything
about the cattle business, then," he
said lightly. "So ask your boss if you
can have three hours off next Friday
and we'll see the werewolf movie."

She hesitated. "Won't it be kind of
gory?"

He sighed. "There's always that cartoon movie that Johnny Depp does the
voice-over for, the chameleon Western."

She laughed. He was pleasant, nice
to look at and had a sense of humor.

And she hadn't been on a date in months. It just might be fun.

"Okay, then," she told him. "I like Johnny Depp in anything, even if it's only his voice. That's a date."

He smiled back. "That's a date," he agreed.

There was a lot to do around a ranch during calving season, and most of the cowboys—and cowgirl—didn't plan on getting much sleep.

Heifers who were calving for the first time were watched carefully. There was also an old mama cow who was known for wandering off and hiding in thickets to calve. Nobody knew why; she just did it. Morie named her Bessy and devoted herself to keeping a careful eye on the old girl.

"Now don't go following that old cow around and forget to watch the others," Darby cautioned. "She can't hide where we won't be able to find her."

"I know that, but she's getting some age on her and there's snow being forecast again," she said worriedly. "What if she got stuck in a drift? If we had a repeat of the last storm, we might not even be able to hunt for her. Hard to ride a horse through snow that's over his head," she added, with a straight face.

He laughed. "I see your point. But you have to consider that this is a big spread, and we've got dozens of mama cows around here. Not to mention, we've got a lot of replacement heifers who are dropping calves for the first time. That's a lot of profit in a recession. Can't afford to lose many."

"I know." Her father had cut his cattle herd because of the rising prices of grain, she recalled, and he was concentrating on a higher-quality bull herd rather than expanding into a cow-calf operation like the one his father, the late Jim Brannt, had built up.

"Dang, it's cold today," Darby said as he finished doctoring one of the seed bulls.

"I noticed." Morie chuckled, pulling her denim coat tighter and buttoning it. She had really good clothes back home, but she'd brought the oldest ones with her, so that she didn't raise any suspicions about her status.

"Better get back to riding that fence line," he added.

"I'm on my way. Just had to pick up my iPod," she said, displaying it in its case. "I can't live without my tunes."

He pursed his lips. "What sort of music do you like?"

"Let's see, country and western, classical, soundtracks, blues . . ."

"All of it, in other words."

She nodded. "I like world music, too. It's fun to listen to foreign artists, even if I mostly can't understand anything they sing."

He shook his head. "I'm just a straight John Denver man."

She lifted both eyebrows.

"He was a folk singer in the sixties," he told her. "Did this one song, 'Calypso,' about that ship that Jacques Cousteau used to drive around the world when he was diving." He smiled with nostalgia. "Dang, I must have spent a small fortune playing that one on jukeboxes." He looked at her. "Don't know what a jukebox is, I'll bet."

"I do so. My mom told me all about them."

He shook his head. "How the world has changed since I was a boy." He sighed. "Some changes are good. Most—" he glowered "—are not."

She laughed. "Well, I like my iPod, because it's portable music." She attached her earphones to the device, with which she could surf the internet, listen to music, even watch movies as long as she was within reach of the Wi-Fi system on the ranch. "I'll see you later."

"Got a gun?" he asked suddenly.

She gaped at him. "What am I going to do, shoot wolves? That's against the law."

"Everything's against the law where ranchers are concerned. No, I wasn't thinking about four-legged varmints. There's an escaped convict, a murderer. They think he's in the area."

She caught her breath. "Could he get onto the ranch?"

"No fence can keep out a determined man. He'll just go right over it," he told her. He went back into the bunkhouse and returned with a small handgun in a leather holster. "It's a .32 Smith & Wesson," he said, handing it up. He made a face when she hesitated. "You don't have to kill a man to scare him. Just shoot near him and run." He frowned. "Can you shoot a gun?"

"Oh, yes, my dad made sure of it," she told him. "He taught me and my brother to use anything from a pea-shooter to all four gauges of shotguns."

He nodded. "Then take it. Put it in your saddlebag. I'll feel better."

She smiled at him. "You're nice, Darby."

"You bet I am," he replied. "Can't afford to lose someone who works as hard as you do."

She made a face at him. She mounted her horse, a chestnut gelding, and rode off.

The open country was so beautiful. In the distance she could see the Teton Mountains, rising like white spires against the gray, overcast sky. The fir trees were still a deep green, even in the last frantic clutches of fading winter. It was too soon for much tender vegetation to start pushing up out of the ground, but spring was close at hand.

Most ranchers bred their cattle to drop calves in early spring, just as the grass came out of hibernation and grain crops began growing. Lush, fresh grass would be nutritious to feed the cows while they nursed their offspring. By the time the calves were weaned, the grass would still be lush and green and tasty for them, if the rain cooperated.

She liked the way the Kirk boys worked at ecology, at natural systems. They had windmills everywhere to pump water into containers for the cattle. They grew natural grasses and were careful not to strain the delicate topsoil by overplanting. They used crop rotation to keep the soil fresh and productive, and they used natural fertilizer. They maintained ponds of cattle waste, which was used to produce methane that powered electricity for the calving barn and the other outbuildings. It was a high-tech, fascinating sort of place. Especially for a bunch of cattlemen who'd taken a dying ranch and made it grow and thrive. They weren't rich yet, but they were well-to-do and canny about the markets. Besides that, Mallory was something of a financial genius. The ranch was starting to make money. Big money.

Cane went to the cattle shows with their prize bulls, Darby had told her, when Cane stayed sober for a long-enough stretch. He was sort of intimidating to Morie, but he had a live-wire personality and he could charm buyers.

Dalton, whom they called, for some reason, Tank, was the marketing specialist. He drew up brochures for the production sales, traveled to conferences and conventions, attended political-action committee meetings for the county and state and even national cattlemen's associations, and devoted himself to publicizing the ranch's prize cattle. He worked tirelessly. But he was a haunted man, and it showed.

Mallory was the boss. He made all the big decisions, although he was democratic enough to give his brothers a voice. They were all opinionated. Darby said it was genetic; their parents had been the same.

Morie understood that. Her dad was one of the most opinionated men she'd ever known. Her mother was gentle and sweet, although she had a temper. Life at home had always been interesting. It was just that Morie had become an entrée for any money-hungry bachelor looking for financial stability. Somewhere there must be a man who'd want her for what she was, not what she had.

She rode the fence line, looking for breaks. It was one of the important chores around the ranch. A fence that was down invited cattle to cross over onto public lands, or even onto the long two-lane state highway that ran beside the ranch. One cow in the road could cause an accident that would result in a crippling lawsuit for the brothers.

Darby had been vocal about the sue-everybody mentality that had taken over the country in recent years. He told Morie that in his day, attorneys were held to a higher standard of behavior and weren't even allowed to advertise their services. Nobody had sued anybody that he knew of, when he was a boy. Now people sued over everything. He had little respect for the profession today. Morie had defended it. Her uncle was a superior court judge who'd been a practicing attorney for many years. He was honest to a fault and went out of his way to help people who'd been wronged and didn't have money for an attorney. Darby had conceded that perhaps there were some good lawyers. But he added that frivolous lawsuits were going to end civilization as it stood. She just smiled and went on about her business. They could agree to disagree. After all, tolerance was what made life bearable.

She halted at the creek long enough to let her gelding have a drink. She adjusted her earphones so that she could listen to Mark Mancina's exquisite soundtrack for the motion picture *August Rush.* There was an organ solo that sent chills of delight down her spine. She got the same feeling listen-

ing to Bach's Toccata and Fugue in D
Minor played on a pipe organ. Music
was a big part of her life. She could
play classical piano, but she was rusty.
College had robbed her of practice
time. She'd noticed a big grand piano
in the Kirks' living room. She wondered
which of the brothers played. She'd
never asked.

She stopped at a stretch of fence
where the last snow-and-ice storm had
brought a limb down. The ice was gone,
but the limb was still resting on the
fence, bending it down so that cattle
could have walked over it. The limb was
a big one, but she was strong. She dismounted, buttoned her coat pocket so
that the iPod wouldn't fall out and went
at the limb.

She had to break pieces off before
she could ease it onto the ground. In
the process, one of the sharp branches
cut her cheek. She muttered as she felt
blood on her fingers when she touched
it. Well, it would mend.

She pushed the limb onto the ground
with a grimace, but she was glad to see
that the fence wasn't damaged, only a

little bent from the collision. She wrangled it back into some sort of order and made a note on the iPod so that she could report its location to the brothers with the GPS device she always carried with her. They were pretty high-tech for a low-budget operation, she thought. They had laptops that they used during roundup to coordinate all the activity.

She paused as the crescendo built on the soundtrack, and closed her eyes to savor it. How wonderful it must be, she thought, to be a composer and be able to write scores that touched the very heart and soul of listeners. She was musical, but she had no such talent. She didn't compose. She only interpreted the music of others when she played the piano or, less frequently, the guitar.

"Hurt yourself?" A deep, drawling voice came from behind.

She whirled, her heart racing, her eyes wide and shocked as she faced a stranger standing a few feet away. She looked like a doe in the sights of a hunter.

He was tall and lean, with dark eyes and hair under a wide-brimmed hat, wearing jeans and a weather-beaten black hat. He was smiling.

"Mr. Kirk," she stammered, as she finally recognized Dalton Kirk. She hadn't seen him often. He wasn't as familiar to her as Mallory was. "Sorry, I wasn't paying attention . . ."

He reached out and took one of the earphones, pursing his sensual lips as he listened. He handed it back. *"August Rush,"* he said.

Her eyebrows shot up. "You know the score?"

He smiled at her surprise. "Yes. It's one of my own favorites, especially that pipe-organ solo."

"That's my favorite, too," she agreed.

He glanced at the fence. "Make a note of the coordinates so we can replace that section of fence, will you?" he asked. "It will keep the cattle in for now, but not for long."

"I already did," she confirmed. She was still catching her breath.

"There's an escaped convict out here somewhere," he told her. "I don't think he's guilty, but he's desperate. I love music as much as anybody, but there's a time and place for listening to it, and this isn't it. If I'd been that man, and desperate enough to shoot somebody or take a hostage, you'd be dead or taken away by now."

She'd just realized that. She nodded.

"Now you see why it's against the law to listen with earphones when you're driving," he said. "You couldn't hear a siren with those on." He indicated the earphones.

"Yes. I mean, yes, sir."

He cocked his head. His dark eyes twinkled. "Call me Tank. Everybody does."

"Why?" she blurted out.

"We were facing down an Iraqi tank during the invasion of Iraq," he told her, "and we were taking substantial damage. We lost comms with the artillery unit that was covering us and we didn't have an antitank weapon with us." He shrugged. "I waded in with a grenade and the crew surrendered. Ever since, I've been Tank."

She laughed. He wasn't as intimidating as he'd once seemed.

"So keep those earphones in your pocket and listen to music when it's a little safer, will you?"

"I will," she promised, and put away the iPod.

He mounted the black gelding she hadn't heard approaching and rode closer. "That thing isn't a phone, is it?"

"No, sir."

"Do you carry a cell phone?" he added, and his lean, strong face was solemn.

She pulled a little emergency one out of her pocket and showed it to him. "It's just for 911 calls, but it would do the job."

"It wouldn't. We'll get you one. It's essential here. I'll tell Darby—he'll arrange it for you."

"Thanks," she said, surprised. She should have been using her own phone, but she thought it might give her away. It was one of the very expensive models. The one she was carrying looked much more like something a poor cowgirl would own.

"Oh, we're nice," he told her with a straight face. "We have sterling characters, we never curse or complain, we're always easy to get along with. . . ." He stopped because she was muffling laughter.

"Just because Cane can turn the air blue, and Mallory throws things is no reason to think we're not easygoing," he instructed.

"Yes, sir. I'll remember that."

He laughed. "If you need anything, you call," he said. "Keep your eyes open. The man who escaped was charged with killing a man in cold blood," he added solemnly. "Joe Bascomb. He was with me in Iraq. But desperate men can do desperate things. He might hurt a stranger, even a woman, if he thought she might turn him in to the law. He's sworn he'll never go back to jail." His eyes were sad. "I never thought he'd run. I'm sure he didn't mean to kill the other man, if in fact he did. But they're bound and determined to catch him, and he's determined not to be caught. So you watch your back."

"I'll be more careful."

"Please do. Good help is hard to find." He tipped his hat, and rode away.

Morie breathed a sigh of relief and got back on her horse.

CHAPTER THREE

There was some big shindig planned for the following Friday, Morie heard. The housekeeper, Mavie Taylor, was vocal about the food the brothers wanted prepared for it.

"I can't make canapés," she groaned, pushing back a graying strand of hair that had escaped its bun. She propped her hands on her thin hips and glowered. "How am I supposed to come up with things like that when all they ever want is steak and potatoes?"

"Listen, canapés are easy," Morie said gently. "You can take a cocktail sausage and wrap it in bacon, secure it with a toothpick and bake it." She gave the temperature setting and cooking time. "Then you can make little cucumber sandwiches cut into triangles, tea cakes, cheese straws . . ."

"Wait a minute." She was writing frantically on a pad. "What else?"

Morie glowed. It was the first time the acid-tongued housekeeper had ever said anything halfway pleasant to her. She named several other small, easily prepared snacks that would be recognizable to any social animal as a canapé.

"How do you know all this?" the woman asked finally, and suspiciously.

"Last ranch I worked at, I had to help in the kitchen," Morie said, and it was no lie. She often helped Shelby when company was coming.

"This is nice," she replied. She tried to smile. It didn't quite work. Those facial muscles didn't get much exercise. "Thanks," she added stiffly.

Morie grinned. "You're welcome."

Her small eyes narrowed. "Okay, what about table linen and stuff?"

"Do you have a selection of those?"

"I hope so." The harassed woman sighed. "I only came to work here a couple of weeks before you did. I've never had to cook for a party and I don't have a clue about place settings. I'm no high-society chef! I mean, look at me!" she exclaimed, indicating her sweatpants and T-shirt that read Give Chickens the Vote!

Morie tried not to giggle. She'd never credited the Kirks' venomous housekeeper with a sense of humor. Perhaps she'd misjudged the woman.

"I cooked for a bunkhouse crew before this," Mavie muttered. "The brothers knew it . . . I told them so. Now here they come wanting me to cook for visiting politicians from Washington and figure out how to put priceless china and delicate crystal and silver utensils in some sort of recognizable pattern on an antique linen tablecloth!"

"It's all right," Morie said. "I'll help."

She blinked. "You will? They won't like it." She nodded toward the distant living room.

"They won't know," she promised.

The housekeeper shifted nervously. "Okay. Thanks. That Bruner woman's always in here complaining about how I cook," she added sourly.

"That's all right, she's always complaining about how I dress."

The other woman's eyes actually twinkled. Nothing made friends like a common enemy. "She thinks I'm not capable of catering a party. She wants to hire one of her society friends and let Mallory pay her a fortune to do it."

"We'll show her," Morie said.

There was a chuckle. "Okay. I'm game. What's next?"

Morie spent a very enjoyable hour of her free time laying out a menu for Mavie and diagramming the placement of the silver and crystal on the tablecloth. She advised buying and using a transparent plastic cover over the antique tablecloth to preserve it from spills of red wine, which, the housekeeper groaned, the brothers preferred.

"They'll never let me do that." She sighed.

"Well, I suppose not," Morie replied,

trying to imagine her mother, that superhostess, putting plastic on her own priceless imported linen. "And I suppose we can find a dry cleaner who can get out stains if they're fresh."

"I don't guess I can wear sweats to serve at table," Mavie groaned.

"You could hire a caterer" came the suggestion.

"Nearest caterer I know of is in Jackson, ninety miles away," the housekeeper said. "Think they'll spring to fly him and his staff down here?"

Morie chuckled. No, not in the current economic environment. "Guess not."

"Then we'll have to manage." She frowned. "I do have one passable dress. I guess it will still fit. And I can get a couple of the cowboys' wives to come and help. But I don't know how to serve anything."

"I do," Morie said gently. "I'll coach you and the wives who help."

Mavie cocked her head. Her blue eyes narrowed. "You're not quite what you seem, are you?"

Morie tried to look innocent. "I just cooked for a big ranch," she replied.

The housekeeper pursed her lips. "Okay. If you say so."

Morie grinned. "I do. So, let's talk about entrées!"

Mallory came in while Morie was sipping a cup of coffee with Mavie after their preparations.

Morie looked up, disturbed, when Mallory stared at her pointedly.

"It's my afternoon off," she blurted.

His thick eyebrows lifted. "Did I say anything?"

"You were thinking it," she shot back.

"Hard worker and reads minds." Mallory nodded. "Nice combination."

"She gave me some tips on canapés for that high-society party you're making me cook for," Mavie grumbled, glaring at him. "Never cooked for any darn politicians. I don't like politicians." She frowned. "I wonder what hemlock looks like . . . ?"

"You stop that," Mallory said at once. "We're feeding them so we can push some agendas their way. We need a sympathetic ear in Washington for the cattlemen's lobby."

"They should keep buffalo in the park where they belong instead of letting them wander onto private land and infect cattle with brucellosis," Morie muttered. "And people who don't live here shouldn't make policy for people who do. They're trying to force out all the independent ranchers and farmers, it seems to me."

Mallory pulled up a chair and sat down. "Exactly," he said. "Mavie, can I have coffee, please?"

"Sure thing, boss." She jumped up to make more.

"Another thing is this biofuel," Mallory said. "Sure, it's good tech. It will make the environment better. We're already using wind and sun for power, even methane from animal waste. But we're growing so much corn for fuel that we're risking precious food stores. We've gone to natural, native grasses to feed our cattle because corn prices are killing our budget."

"Grass fed is better," Morie replied.

"Especially for consumers who want lean cuts of beef."

He glowered at her. "We don't run beef cattle."

"You run herd bulls," she pointed out. "Same end result. You want a bull who breeds leaner beef calves."

Mallory shifted uncomfortably. "We don't raise veal."

"Neither do—" She stopped abruptly. She was about to say "we," because her father wouldn't raise it, either. "Neither do a lot of ranchers. You must have a good model for your breeding program."

"We do. I studied animal husbandry in school," he said. "I learned how to tweak the genetics of cattle to breed for certain traits."

"Like lower birth weight in calves and leaner conformation."

"Yes. And enlarged . . ." He stopped in midsentence and seemed uncomfortable. "Well, for larger, uh, seed storage in herd bulls."

She had to bite her tongue to keep from bursting out laughing. It was a common reference among cattlemen, but he was uncomfortable using the term with her. He was very old-world. She didn't laugh. He was protecting her, in a sense. She shouldn't like it. But she did.

He was studying her with open curiosity. "You know a lot about the cattle business."

"I pick up a lot, working ranches," she said. "I always listened when the boss talked about improving his herd."

"Was he a good boss?"

"Oh, yes," she said. Her dad had a very low turnover in his employees. He was fair to them, made sure they had insurance and every other benefit he could give them.

"Why did you leave, then?" he asked.

She shifted. Had to walk a careful line on this one, she thought. "I had a little trouble with an admirer," she said finally. It was true. The man hadn't been a ranch hand, but she insinuated that he was.

Mallory's eyes narrowed. "That won't ever happen here. You have problems with any of the cowboys, you just tell me. I'll handle it."

She beamed. "Thanks."

"No problem. Thanks, Mavie," he added when the housekeeper put a cup of black coffee with just a little cream at his hand. "You make the best coffee in Wyoming."

"You're only saying that because you want an apple pie for supper."

His eyebrows shot up. "Hell, am I that obvious?"

"Absolutely," she declared.

He shrugged. "I love apple pie."

"I noticed. I suppose I can peel apples and listen while you two talk cattle," she said, and got up to retrieve fresh apples from the counter along with a big bowl and a paring knife.

"Uh, about men," Morie said, looking for an opening.

He scowled. "You are having problems here!"

"No!" She swallowed. "No, I'm not. There's this nice man in town who wants to go out with me. His father runs the local tractor store—"

"No!"

She gaped at him.

"Clark Edmondson has a bad reputation locally," he continued curtly. "He took out one of Jack Corrie's daughters and deserted her at a country bar when she wouldn't make out with him in his car. He was pretty drunk at the time."

"We're not going to a bar," she stammered uncharacteristically, "just to a movie in town."

He cocked his head. "What movie?"

"That cartoon one, about the chameleon. The lizard Western."

"Actually, that one's pretty good. I would have thought he'd prefer the werewolf movie, though."

She shifted in her chair. "That's the first one he suggested. I don't like gore. The reviewers said it had some in it, and it got bad reviews."

"You believe reviewers know what they're talking about?" he queried with a twinkle in his eyes. "They don't buy books or movie tickets, you know. They're just average people with average opinions. One opinion doesn't make or break a sale in the entertainment business."

"I never thought of it like that."

"I don't read reviews. I look at what a book is about, or a movie, and make up my own mind whether to read it or see it in a theater. In fact, the werewolf movie had exquisite cinematography and some of the best CGI I've seen in a long time. I liked it, especially that gorgeous blonde girl in that red, red cape in the white, snowy background," he recalled. "Film reviewers. What do they know?" he scoffed.

"Opinionated, is what he is," Mavie said from beside them, where she sat peeling apples. "And it was Bill Duvall who told you about the Corrie girl. He's sweet on her and she doesn't like Clark, so you take that into account when you hear the story." She looked down at her hands working on an apple. "Nothing wrong with Clark, except he's flighty. You don't understand flighty, because all three of you are rock-solid sort of people, full of opinions and attitude."

Mallory let out a short laugh as he sipped coffee. "I don't have an attitude."

"Oh, yes, you do," the housekeeper shot back.

He shrugged. "Maybe I do." He glanced at Morie and his eyes narrowed. "You take your cell phone with you, and if Clark gets out of hand, you call. Got that?"

"Oh . . . okay." It was like being back at home. He sounded just like her dad did when she'd dated a boy he didn't know in high school. "He wanted to take me to the movies on Saturday, but I'm supposed to be watching calving. . . ."

"I'll get one of the part-timers to come in and cover for you. This time," he added curtly. "Don't expect concessions. We can't afford them."

She flushed. "Yes, sir. Thanks."

"She's over twenty-one, boss," Mavie said drily.

"She works for me," he replied. "I'm responsible for every hire I've got. Some more than others." He looked pointedly at Morie, and he didn't look away.

It was like being caught by a live wire when she met that searching stare. Her heart kicked into high gear. Her breath caught in her throat. She felt the intensity of the look right down to her toes. She'd never felt such a surge of pleasure in her whole life.

Mallory appeared to forcibly drag his eyes away. He sipped coffee. "Well, you can go, but you be careful. I still think he's a risk. But it's your life."

"Yes, it is," she replied. Her throat felt tight, and she was flushed. She got to her feet. "Thanks for the coffee," she told the housekeeper. "It's time for me to get to work."

"Don't fall in the dipping pool," Mallory said with a straight face, but his dark eyes twinkled in a way that was new and exciting.

"Yes, sir, boss," she replied. She smiled and turned to move quickly out of the room before she embarrassed herself by staring at him. She wondered how she was going to conceal the sudden new delight she got from looking at her boss.

She had a nice pair of slacks and a pink-and-lime embroidered sweater. She wore those for her date, and let her long hair down. She brushed it until it shone. It was thick and black and beautiful, like her mother's. When she looked in the mirror, she saw many traces of her mother in her own face. She wasn't beautiful, but she wasn't plain, either. She had the same elfin features that had taken Shelby Kane Brannt to such fame in her modeling days. And Morie's grandmother, Maria Kane, had been a motion-picture star, quite famous for her acting ability. Morie hadn't inherited that trait. Her one taste of theater in college had convinced her that she was never meant for the stage.

She had a lightweight denim coat, and she wore that over her sweater, because it was cold outside. The weather was fluctuating madly. Typical Wyoming weather, she thought amusedly. The Texas climate was like that, too.

She heard a car drive up to the bunkhouse. She whipped her fanny pack into place and went out to meet Clark. He was sitting behind the wheel of the sports car, grinning.

She noted that he didn't get out to open her door. He leaned across and threw it open for her.

She climbed in. "Hi."

"Hi, back. Ready for a nice movie?"

"You bet."

He put the car in gear and roared out down the driveway.

"Don't do that," she groaned. "We have heifers calving in the barn!"

"Oops, sorry, didn't think," he said, but he didn't look concerned. "They'll get over it. Nice night. They said it might snow, but I don't believe the forecast. They're mostly wrong."

She was thinking about the nervous heifers being kept up because it was their first breeding season, and wondering how much flak she was going to get from her boss if anything happened because of Clark's thoughtlessness.

"Stop worrying," he teased. "It's just cows, for heaven's sake."

Just cows. She loved to stop and pet them when she was in the barn. She loved their big eyes and big noses, and the soft fur between their eyes. They were so gentle. And these little heifers, even if they were animals, must be so scared. She'd always had a terror of childbirth, for reasons she could never quite understand. It was one of many reasons that she was hesitant to marry at all.

"Do you know that Elizabeth the First never married and never had a child?" she remarked.

He made a face. "History. I hate that. Let's talk about who's leading the pack in *American Idol!*"

She gaped at him. She didn't watch television very much. "I watch the Weather Channel, the military channel and the science channels mostly," she remarked. "I've never watched any of those audience-participation shows."

"I can see that we're never going to meet in the middle on issues," he re-marked. "Doesn't matter. You're cute and I like you. We can go from there."

Could they? She wondered.

The movie was fun. It was clever and funny and both of them came out of the theater smiling.

"Now let's have some nice Chinese food," he said. "You hungry?"

"Starved. But we're going Dutch," she added firmly. "I bought my own movie ticket . . . I'll pay for my food, too."

His eyebrows arched. "I wouldn't expect you to owe me anything if I bought dinner."

She smiled. "Just the same, I like everything on an equal footing."

"You're a strange girl," he commented thoughtfully.

"Strange?" She shrugged. "I suppose I am."

"Let's eat."

He led the way into the restaurant and they followed the waitress to a table in a corner.

"This is beautiful," Morie remarked, loving the Asian decor, which featured nice copies of ancient statues and some wood carvings that were very expensive. Morie, who'd traveled Asia, appreciated the culture depicted. She'd loved the people she met in her travels.

"Junk," he told her casually. "Nothing valuable in here."

"I meant that it was pretty," she clarified.

"Oh." He glanced around. "I guess so. A little gaudy for my taste."

She was about to respond when her eye caught movement at the door. There, at the counter, was her boss, Mallory Kirk, with Gelly Bruner. He spoke to the waitress and let her seat them nearby.

He smiled coolly and nodded at Morie and Clark. She was thinking that it was an odd coincidence, having him show up here. Certainly he wouldn't have had any reason to be spying on her. . . .

"Do you believe this?" Clark asked, shocked. "Does he do this every time you go out with a man? I've heard of possessive employers, but this takes the cake."

"He takes his date all over the place," she replied, trying to sound casual. "This is the only really good restaurant in town."

"I suppose so."

"He wouldn't have any reason to keep an eye on me," she pointed out. "I'm just the hired help."

He pursed his lips and studied her. "Sure."

Mallory was looking at her, too, his dark eyes on the long wealth of thick black hair that hung straight and shiny down her back almost to her waist.

"Why are you staring at her?" Gelly asked coldly. "She's just a common person. She works for you. And why are we here? You know I hate Chinese food!"

He didn't hear her. He was thinking that he'd never seen anything as beautiful as that long black hair. It brought to mind a poem. She'd probably be familiar with it, too—Bess, the landlord's black-eyed daughter, plaiting a dark red love knot into her long, black hair. "The Highwayman" by Alfred Noyes. It was a tragic poem, the heroine sacrificing herself for the hero. "'I'll come to thee by moonlight, though hell should bar the way . . .'"

"What?" Gelly asked blankly.

He hadn't realized that he'd spoken aloud. "Nothing. What would you like to order?" he added and forced himself to look at his date and not Morie.

Morie was uncomfortable. Clark wanted to talk about contestants on the television show, and she had no point of reference at all.

"That guy, you know, he really can't sing, but he's got a following and he's getting most of the votes," he muttered. "I like the girl. She's classy, she's got a great voice . . . Are you listening?"

She grimaced. "Sorry. I was thinking about the weather reports. They think we might have another snow, and we've got a lot of first-time mothers dropping calves."

"Cows," he groaned. "Morie, there's more to life than four-legged steaks."

Her eyes widened. "Mr. Kirk doesn't have a cow-calf operation. It's strictly a seed-bull ranch."

He blinked. "Seed bull."

"Yes. They produce industry-leading bulls for market." She leaned forward. "They don't eat them."

He shook his head. "You are the odd-est girl I ever met."

She grinned. "Why, thank you!"

He picked up his wineglass and had a long sip. "Sure you don't want any wine?" he asked. "This is the only res-taurant in town where you can buy sin-gle drinks legally."

"I can't drink," she said. "Bad stom-ach. I get very sick. Can't drink carbon-ated beverages, either. Just coffee or iced tea. Or, in this case—" she lifted the little cup with steaming green tea "—hot tea." She sipped it and closed her eyes. "Wonderful!"

He made a face. "You didn't put sugar in it."

"Oh, nobody puts sugar in it in Ja-pan," she blurted out and then bit her tongue. "At least, from what I've read," she corrected quickly.

"I can't drink it straight. It tastes aw-ful." He put the wineglass down. "They have good desserts here, sticky rice with mango or coconut ice cream."

"The ice cream," she said, laughing. "I love it."

"Me, too." He motioned to the waitress. "At least we both like one thing," he mused.

When they got ready to leave, Mallory Kirk watched them through narrowed eyes. He got up while Morie was paying the bill and motioned Clark to one side.

Clark gave him a nervous look. "Mr. Kirk," he said pleasantly enough.

Mallory's dark eyes narrowed. "She's not young enough to be my daughter, but I'm responsible for her. If you do anything she doesn't like," he added with the coldest smile Clark had ever seen, "I'll pay you a visit."

"You can't threaten people," Clark began, flushed.

"Oh, it's no threat, son," Mallory said. His jaw tautened. "It's an ironclad, gold-edged promise."

He turned and walked off, pausing at his table to leave a tip and help Gelly to her feet.

Clark escorted an oblivious Morie out to his car. He was flushed from the wine and angry that one of the Kirk brothers had threatened him.

"I should call the police," he muttered as he started the car and roared off out of the parking lot.

"What for?" Morie asked, curious.

"Your boss made a threat," he said stiffly.

"My boss? What are you talking about?"

He started to tell her and then thought better of it. She was pretty and he liked her; he didn't want her to think there was a reason for her boss to warn him off.

He shrugged. "He just said I'd better look after you," he amended.

Her dark eyebrows arched. "Why in the world would he say something like that?" she asked, and tried not to look as flattered as she felt. No man interfered in a woman's life unless he liked her.

"Beats me." He glanced at her. "He's not stuck on you, is he?"

She burst out laughing. "Oh, sure, he likes me because I've got millions in a trust fund and I know all the best people," she said drily.

He laughed, too. He was out of his mind. She wasn't the sort of woman a cattle baron would want to marry. The Kirks had fabulous parties with all sorts of famous people attending them to sell those cattle she talked about. They had some incredibly well-known friends, apparently. But Morie dressed in old clothes, even for a date. She was clueless. He was overreacting. Maybe Mallory really did feel responsible for her. Maybe he knew her folks. He might be afraid of a lawsuit. It wasn't anything personal. Just good business.

"Well, I loved the movie," she said. "Thanks."

"Thank you. I don't get out as much as I'd like to," he added. "But we could see a movie once in a while and have dinner out, if you like."

She smiled. "I'll think about that."

He'd planned to take her to an overlook that doubled as the local lover's lane. But after Mallory's blunt speech, he wasn't keen to push the man. So instead, he drove her back to the ranch.

He even turned off the engine and walked her to the door of the bunkhouse.

"You live in there with all those men?" he asked curiously.

"I have my own room," she explained. "They're nice men."

"If you say so."

"Well, thanks again," she said, hesitating.

He smiled. He liked that little nervous laugh, the way her lips turned up at the corners, the faint dimple beside her mouth.

He bent and drew his lips gently against hers.

She tolerated the kiss. But she didn't react to it. She felt nothing. Nothing at all.

He noticed that. They were too different to settle in together. But she was cute and he liked company on a night out.

"We'll do it again soon," he said.

She smiled. "Sure."

She turned around and went into the bunkhouse. Darby was sitting by the door, his eyebrows arching as she walked in and closed the door behind her.

"Have fun?" he asked in a hushed tone, so he didn't wake the cowboys down the hall.

"Yes. I guess."

He tilted his head. "You guess?"

"Boss showed up at the restaurant," she said, and looked puzzled. "I didn't know he liked Chinese food."

Darby's eyes almost popped. "He hates it."

She hesitated. "Well, he had Ms. Bruner with him. Maybe she likes it."

"Maybe."

"You sleep good, Darby."

"You, too," he said gently.

"The heifers doing okay?" she asked.

"Doing fine. We'll just hope and pray that that the weatherman's wrong on that snow forecast."

"I'll agree with that. Good night."

"'Nite."

She went into her room and closed the door. Darby had seemed shocked that the boss went to the restaurant where Morie was eating. She was

shocked, too, but also pleased and flattered and thrilled to death.

She slept, finally. And her dreams
were sweet.

CHAPTER FOUR

The last thing Morie expected the next day was to find a seething Gelly Bruner on her doorstep. Well, at the bunkhouse when she went in for lunch.

"I hate Chinese food," Gelly said without a greeting.

"I'm sorry," Morie said. "In that case, perhaps you should avoid Chinese restaurants." She smiled.

"He went there because of you, didn't he?" she demanded. "To make sure your date knew he was watching out for you."

Morie looked innocent. "Why would he do that? He's not my dad."

Gelly frowned. "He's not your boyfriend, either, and you'd better not make eyes at him," she added coldly. "You won't last long here if you do."

"I work here," Morie pointed out. "That's all."

"You see how they live and you like it," the blonde said, giving Morie's clothing an even colder look. "You're poor and you'd like to have nice things and mingle with the right people."

"I do mingle with the right people," Morie said, offended.

"Cowboys" came the disparaging reply. "Smelly and stupid."

"They're neither."

"If you do anything to make Mallory notice you, I'll make sure it never happens again," she added, lowering her voice. "You won't be the first person I've helped off this ranch. It isn't wise to make an enemy of me."

"I work here," Morie said, growing angry. She had her mother's looks, but her father's fiery temper. "And nobody threatens me."

Gelly shifted. She wasn't used to people who fought back. "My people are well-to-do," she said stiffly. "And you won't like how I get even."

Morie raised an eyebrow. "Ditto."

"Well, you just stay away from Mallory," she said bluntly. "He's mine and I don't share!"

"Does he know?"

Gelly blinked. "Know what?"

"That he belongs to you? Perhaps I should ask him. . . ."

"You shut up!" The blonde woman's fists balled at her sides and her face grew flushed with temper. "I'll get you!"

"Wind and water," Morie said philosophically. "Words."

Gelly drew back her hand and started to slap the younger woman, but Morie threw up her forearm instinctively and blocked the move.

"I have a brown belt in Tae Kwon Do," she told Gelly in a soft voice. Her dark eyes glittered. "Try that again, and you'll wish you hadn't."

Gelly let out a furious sound. "I'll tell Mallory!"

"Be my guest," Morie offered. "I can

teach him a few moves, too, in case you try that with him."

Gelly stomped back off toward the house, muttering to herself.

Morie shook her head at the retreating figure.

"Unwise," Darby said, joining her. He watched Gelly walk away. "She makes a bad enemy. We lost a hand because she accused him of stealing. Told you about that."

"She'll think she's poked a hornet's nest if she tries it with me. Nobody warns me off people and gets away with it," she said curtly. "I don't have any designs on the boss, for God's sake! I don't even know him. I just work here!"

Darby patted her on the shoulder paternally. "There, there, don't let it get you down. Two nights' sleep and you'll forget why you argued with her. Come on in and eat. We've got chili and Mexican corn bread that Mavie made for us. She's a wonderful cook."

"Yes, she is," Morie agreed. She grimaced. "Sorry. I don't usually lose my temper, but she set me off. What a piece of work!"

"I do agree. But she's the boss's headache, not ours, thank God."

"I suppose so."

She followed him inside.

But that wasn't the end of it. Mallory called Morie up to the big house, and he wasn't smiling as he motioned her into the living room and closed the door.

"Sit down, please." He indicated a leather chair, not the cushy brocade-covered white sofa. Her jeans were stained with grass and mud from helping with calving. Probably he didn't want a brown-spotted couch, she thought wickedly.

She sat. "Yes, sir?"

He paced. "Gelly said that you threatened her."

"Did she?" She sounded amazed. "How odd."

He turned and stared down at her with piercing dark eyes. "I'd like to hear your side of the story before I decide what to do."

She cocked her head and studied him. "I'll tell you, if you're sure you want to know, boss. But I won't sugarcoat it, even though I need this job."

He seemed surprised. "Okay. That's a deal. Shoot."

"She warned me off you," she said simply. "Then she threatened to have me fired. Finally, she tried to slap me and I blocked the move. She left and I went back to work."

"In between, there's some stuff missing," he pointed out. "Like what you said that made her try to slap you."

"She said that I was after you because you were rich and I was poor," she added. The words did sting, despite Morie's background. "She also said cowboys were smelly and stupid and that she could get me fired if she liked. I told her that I didn't like threats and that perhaps I should ask you if you were her personal property. That's when she tried to slap me."

He just stared at her. He didn't speak. God knew what Gelly had actually told him about the incident.

"I've never known her to get physical

with anyone," he returned. "She was crying."

"Oh, gee, I'm sorry," Morie said with cutting sarcasm. "Start a fight and lose it and then go crying to some big, strong man to make it all right. That how it goes?"

His jaw tautened. "I'm the boss."

"Yes, you are, sir," she agreed. "So if you want to fire me, go right ahead. There are a few ranches where I haven't tried to get work yet. I'm willing to give them a try."

He let out an angry sigh. "You might just admit that you were wrong and apologize to her," he said curtly.

"Apologize when I was defending myself from an attack?" she asked. "How does that work, exactly?"

"She said you started it."

"And I say that she did."

He looked even angrier. "She's a socialite. You're a hired hand on my ranch. That's what makes the difference."

"I get it." She nodded, trying to contain her temper. "It's the class thing, right? She's rich and I'm poor, so she's right."

"You work for me, damn it!" he shot back. "And you're that close—" he held up his forefinger and thumb a fraction apart "—to not working for me!"

Her small hands balled up at her sides. "Nobody throws a punch at me and gets away with it. I don't care who she is! If she'd landed that blow, I'd have had her prosecuted and I'd call every damned newspaper and television station in Wyoming to make sure everybody knew what she did!"

His eyes were glittering. "She said you told her that you wanted me and you were going to get me, and she'd be out in the cold!"

She rolled her eyes. "Good grief, you're almost old enough to be my father," she burst out. "What in the world was she thinking?"

He had been pacing while they talked, but as she spoke her last sentence, he'd stopped and stared at her. Then he moved like greased lightning toward her.

His mouth came down on hers with a pressure and skill that shocked her speechless. While she was trying to decide on a course of action, he backed her up against the wall between two landscape paintings, lifted her and braced his body against hers. The kiss was, at first, a medium of his anger. And then, quite suddenly, it was something entirely different.

She felt one big, warm hand high on her hip, his long leg insinuating itself between both of hers. He shifted, so that she felt him intimately. He was aroused and apparently not shy about sharing the fact with her. His mouth eased and became persuasive, teasing her lips apart while his hand positioned her slender hips so that he could get even closer.

She shivered. No man had ever made such a sudden, sensual pass at her, and she'd never felt such a surge of utter and absolute pleasure at physical contact.

But when the contact grew even more intimate, and she felt her body urging her to help him with that zipper he was trying to undo, she came to her senses.

She dragged her mouth out from un-

der his with reluctance. "No!" she whispered. "No, don't!"

She pushed at his chest weakly. If he
insisted, she wasn't sure that she could
stop him. She didn't want to stop
him. . . .

He was out of his mind with the pleasure. He hadn't felt it in years, certainly
not with Gelly, who was something of a
cold fish, despite her flirting. Morie had
made a sharp remark about his age
and it had hit him in a sore place. But
this was insane. He was taking advantage of the hired help!

He dragged himself away from her
and looked down. She was flushed and
shaking. But it wasn't from fear. He
knew women. She was as aroused as
he was. She hadn't protested the kissing, but she wasn't willing to go further.
She behaved as if she'd never had a
man. He frowned. Could there be a virgin left in the world? Sometimes he
doubted it.

"I'm not an old man," he said angrily.

She was still trying to get her breath.
"Oh, no, you're definitely not old," she
managed. She could taste him on her

mouth, smell the woodsy cologne he wore on her clothing.

He averted his eyes. He didn't lose control of himself, ever. This was embarrassing. "Sorry," he said stiffly.

She swallowed. "It's okay. But I should go back to work now."

"Yes, you should."

She moved away from the wall, hoping she wasn't more disheveled than she felt, and that Mavie wouldn't be around to see her when she left.

He didn't say a word. He watched her go, stiff and uncomfortable, and pondered Gelly's remark that Morie was a rounder who was looking for a rich sugar daddy. He knew that wasn't true. She might be poor. She might even have designs on him for his wealth—it wouldn't be the first time. But she was innocent. He'd have bet the ranch on it.

Morie avoided the other cowboys when she went riding fence lines. She hoped she didn't look as disconcerted and unsettled as she felt. The boss had kissed her. No, she corrected, that hadn't been a kiss. That had been something a lot more overt and sensual. She'd been saucy and deliberately provocative. She'd taunted the sleeping bear, but she hadn't expected such a response.

Her mouth still tingled from the kiss. He might not be the handsomest man around, but he knew exactly what to do with a woman. She hadn't wanted him to stop. That would have been a disaster. He might have wanted her side of the story, but it was obvious that he believed part of Gelly's story. He wanted Morie to apologize to that blond shark, did he? Well, hell would freeze over first. She was the injured party. Gelly should apologize, not her.

But Gelly was the woman in his life. She was wealthy and pretty and cultured. Morie had the same background, but she didn't dare admit it. She couldn't keep her job if the boss knew who her family was.

Which brought to mind another small problem. The boss was having a gala party on Saturday. Morie had been helping Mavie with recipes and tips on serving and place settings and even decorations. Mavie wanted her to help make the canapés. She'd even asked the boss, so Morie was in something of a spot.

As long as she could hide in the kitchen during the festivities, it would be all right. But her family traveled in the same social circles that the Kirk brothers did. It was possible, even probable, that there would be someone at that party who would recognize her. She couldn't let that happen. She'd gone to a lot of trouble to get this job, mainly because she wanted to prove to her parents and herself that she could make it in the world on her own, with no money and no influence. There was also the question of not being pursued for her wealth by some fortune-hunting male on the make.

She wasn't going to lose her job. She just had to stay out of sight in the kitchen. If she refused to help Mavie, that would lead to questions she couldn't answer. She agreed. But she was going to wear a kerchief over her hair and an overall and keep hidden.

She only hoped none of the guests were comfortable enough to come in and speak to the cook. That wasn't likely, though. Of course it wasn't.

The big house was ablaze with lights, inside and out. The weather was perfect. It was a beautiful spring night, the temperature was unusually comfortable and guests wandered around inside and out nibbling on canapés and drinking the best imported champagne.

Mavie was fascinated by the people she and her hired staff were feeding. "Did you see that movie star?" she exclaimed. "I just watched his last film, and now he's got a series on one of the pay-per-view channels. Isn't he gorgeous?"

Morie peered out and chuckled. She knew the man, who was sweet and unaffected by his great fame. "He's a doll," she said.

"There's that soccer star who's paid millions a year," Mavie continued. "And that's the president of one of those desert countries overseas!"

"Philippe Sabon," Morie blurted out

without thinking. Her father knew the man, whose wife was from Texas.

Mavie glanced at her suspiciously.

"I read about him in the newspapers," Morie covered quickly. "What a story! He's even more handsome in person!"

Mavie gave an emphatic nod. "Yes, he sure is."

"We'd better get back to work," Morie groaned. "Look at how fast those trays are going down!"

"Good thing we've got plenty of raw material in here." Mavie chuckled.

They worked steadily for the next hour, making and baking succulent treats for the guests. The band was playing some lazy blues tunes, and a few couples were dancing in the big family room by the patio door.

"You should be in there dancing and having fun," Mavie said. "You're young enough to enjoy these parties."

Morie gaped at her. "I'm the hired help."

"Baloney. The boss doesn't think like that."

"Want to bet?" Morie murmured under her breath. She'd already had an unforgettable taste of the boss's attitude toward the lower classes. It had a sting.

Mavie glanced her way. "You want to watch that Gelly person. She was raging to the boss about how you talked to her like a dog and said she was a useless person."

"I said no such thing!" Morie replied indignantly.

"Just telling you what she's saying" came the soft reply. "I've seen women like her all my life. They purr when they're around the man in charge and claw when they're not. She isn't as wealthy as she makes herself out to be. One of my friends works for her folks, and gets paid nothing, not even minimum. She says they put on airs and pretend to be rich, but they're barely middle class. Gelly's hoping for a rich husband to prop up the family finances. She's got her eye on the boss."

"If he's nuts enough to marry her, he'll get what he deserves," Morie pointed out. "That woman has more sharp edges than a razor's blade."

She nodded in agreement. "I think she does, too."

It was almost ten o'clock. The staff would leave soon, and so would most of the guests. Morie would be glad to see her bed. She'd been on her feet since daylight. She was half-starved, as well, because she hadn't had a dinner break. Neither had Mavie.

"I'm so hungry." Morie sighed.

"Me, too. We'll save a few canapés for ourselves," she said, laughing. "I'll put some on a plate for you to take back to your room."

"Thanks, Mavie."

"No, thank you," she replied. "You're a wonderful little worker. I couldn't have managed this alone."

She grinned. "I like working in the kitchen."

"Me, too. Call me old-fashioned, but I love to cook. . . ."

"Where's that wonderful cook?" came a familiar deep voice from the doorway. A minute later, Morie's uncle Danny Brannt came through the doorway, laughing. He stopped dead when he spotted Morie.

She put her finger to her lips, when Mavie's back was turned, and shook her head frantically.

"Who's the cook?" he repeated, beaming at Mavie. "I just had to thank you for those delicious canapés. It's been a long time since I've tasted anything that good."

"It was me—" Mavie laughed "—but my helper here came up with most of the recipes." She indicated Morie. "She's Morie," she added. "I'm Mavis, but everyone calls me Mavie."

"I'm happy to meet you," he said. "Both of you." But when he looked at Morie his eyebrows lifted. "Like working here, do you?" he asked her.

"Oh, yes, very much," she replied.

He pursed his lips. "Can I speak with you for a minute?" he added. "I want to ask you something about that little sausage canapé. For my housekeeper," he said.

"Sure," she replied.

He walked to the back door, held it open and let her go out before him.

She worried that it might make Mavie suspicious, but she had to make him understand. She explained what she was doing.

"What the devil are you up to?" he asked seriously. "Your dad would have a fit if he knew you were working for wages on a ranch!"

"You can't tell him," she replied firmly. "I'm going to show him that I can make it on my own. He doesn't have to like it. But if you tell him where I am, he'll come up here and make trouble. He'll be telling the boss what I can and can't be expected to do and it will ruin everything. You know how he is."

"I guess I do." He frowned. "How did you get a job way up here?"

"A friend of a friend told me they were hiring. And what are you doing here?" she exclaimed.

"I met Cane during a trial. He was a friend of the plaintiff, a land case I heard in superior court in Texas. We had lunch and became friends. Good heavens, I had no idea I'd come to his party and find my niece cooking for it!"

She laughed. "Well, somebody had

to. Mavie had no clue about canapés and Mom makes the best I ever tasted. So does Aunt Edie and your house-keeper."

"If your dad ever finds out about this . . ."

"He won't. And if he ever does, I'll defend you," she promised confidently.

He shook his head. "You always were a handful, even when you were little."

"And you always loved me anyway, Uncle Danny."

"Yes, I did." He hugged her warmly. "Okay, I guess you know what you're doing. I won't tell Kingston. But there will be a dustup when the truth comes out. You'll have to protect me," he added with a grin.

"You know I will. Thanks."

"What are you doing out here instead of working, Miss Brannt?" Gelly's shrill, angry voice came from the doorway. "You are not to have private conversations with my guests, you little gold dig-ger!"

Danny moved into the light. The woman's attitude toward his niece pricked his temper. He'd already formed an opinion of Gelly Bruner, and it wasn't a good one. "I'm not your guest," he pointed out coldly. "I came to see the Kirks."

She flushed and looked uncertain.

"Why don't you go back to the party and stop trying to micromanage your boyfriend's staff?" he drawled. "Perhaps I should have a word with him. . . ."

"Sorry," Gelly said stiffly and managed a cool smile. "Excuse me, please."

She almost ran off.

Morie was stifling laughter. Her uncle could be as intimidating as her father ever was, even if he was usually the easygoing one of the brothers.

Mavie had stepped over to the doorway after Gelly had raced away. She'd obviously heard every word of the exchange with Gelly. Now her eyes were dancing. "Want to stay? I'll cook for you anytime," she added.

He laughed. "Sorry. I have my own business to take care of. The canapés were really delicious. And thanks for the recipe," he told Morie. "I hope I'll see you again one day."

"Same here," she replied, smiling. "Thanks."

He shrugged. "My pleasure." He gave her a last wave before he went back into the family room.

"Who is he?" Mavie asked her.

"A superior court judge from Texas who's a friend of Cane's, apparently," Morie replied innocently. "He wanted me to tell him how to make those sausages so he could get his housekeeper to make them for a party he's having soon. Imagine that! I got to talk to a real judge!"

"He wasn't bad-looking, either," Mavie said with a grin. "Did you say something to Gelly?" she added worriedly.

"No, I didn't say anything. But you heard what the judge said," she added. "She came out to tell me to stop mingling with her guests and get to work. He said she needed to mind her own business."

"Ha!"

Morie's smile widened. "He's such a nice man. I wish we could keep him."

"Me, too." Mavie looked uneasy. "You'll be in trouble, though."

"I'm always in trouble. Let's clean up and then I want to go to bed."

"I'll just put some of those canapés on the plate for you."

"Thanks."

"You're a great little worker," Mavie returned. "I like having you around."

"That's the nicest thing anyone's said to me in a long time," Morie replied, touched.

Mavie just smiled.

Morie sat in front of her small television and watched an old black-and-white comedy while she ate her canapés. They'd turned out very well. What a surprise to have her uncle show up at the Kirks' party. She wasn't aware that he knew Cane. At least she'd been able to get him to keep her secret from her father. She shuddered to think what King would say to her boss.

She knew her mother hadn't told King Brannt where his daughter was working, or what she was doing. Shelby had mentioned that she'd said Morie had a nice job at a department store but she hadn't said where. What a joke.

Morie couldn't have sold heaters to people living in the Yukon.

It had been several days since Mallory had kissed the breath out of her. He'd been avoiding her ever since. Or she'd been avoiding him. It had been unexpected and shocking, but a delicious little interlude that played over and over in Morie's mind. She'd loved it. But obviously the boss hadn't. It seemed that he wanted to make sure she didn't get any ideas about his interest. He'd made a point of being businesslike every time he spoke to her now. There was no more light teasing or pleasant conversation. It was strictly business.

She finished the last canapé and turned off the television. It was up at dawn for more calving and she was still achy and stiff from helping Darby pull two calves that simply weren't anxious to be born. Their reward was the soft bawling sound the calves made when they were delivered and stood up, wobbling away to be licked clean by their mothers.

It was incredible to help deliver a calf.

The process of birth was fascinating to anyone who worked around livestock. The cycle of life and death was a never-ending one on a ranch.

Morie loved working outdoors, away from the city, away from traffic and regimented life. Here, the time clock was the sun. They got up with it and went to bed with it. They learned how to identify birds by their songs. They learned the subtle weather signs that were lost in electronic prognostication. They were of the earth. It was the most wonderful job going, Morie thought, even if the pay wasn't top scale and the work was mostly physical labor that came with mussed, stained clothing. She wouldn't have traded it to model Paris gowns, and she'd once been offered that opportunity. It had amused and pleased her mother, who wasn't surprised when Morie said she'd rather learn how to rope calves.

Her father would never teach her. Her brother, Cort, got the ranch training. Her primitive dad, who was living in the Stone Age, she often told him, wanted her to be a lady of leisure and do feminine things. She told him that she could work cattle every bit as well as her brother and she wanted to prove it. Her dad just laughed and walked off. Not on his ranch. Not ever.

So she found someone else's ranch to prove it on. She'd gotten her college degree. Her dad should be happy that she'd accomplished at least one thing he'd insisted upon. Now she was going to please herself.

She threw on a nightshirt and a pair of pajama bottoms and climbed into bed. She was asleep in seconds.

The next morning, the boss came down to the barn, where she was feeding out a calf whose mother had been attacked by a pack of wolves. The mother had died and state agencies had been called in to trap the wolves and relocate them.

Mallory looked down at her, with the calf on her knees, and something cold inside him started to melt. She had a tender heart. He loved the picture she made, nursing that calf. But he pulled himself up taut. That couldn't be allowed. He wasn't having any more embarrassing interludes with the hired help that could come back to bite him.

She looked up and saw him watching her. She averted her eyes. "Morning, boss," she said.

"Morning."

His tone wasn't reassuring. She sighed. "I'm in trouble again, I guess."

"Gelly said you put a visitor up to insulting her when she told you to get back to work in the kitchen," he said flatly.

Morie just sighed.

"Well?" he persisted.

"The guy was a superior court judge who wanted my canapé recipe for his housekeeper, so I went outside with him to give it to him," she replied wearily. "Miss Bruner interrupted us, and he was angry at the way she spoke to me. I didn't put him up to anything."

He frowned. "A judge?"

"Well, he said he was," she replied, flushing. She wasn't supposed to know the occupations of his guests.

"I see."

No, you don't, she fumed silently.

You don't see anything. Gelly leads you around by your temper, and you let her.

He hesitated. "The canapés were very good."

"Thanks. Mavie and I worked hard."

"Yes." His dark eyes narrowed. "How is it," he continued suspiciously, "that you know so much about how to organize a high-society party? And just where did you learn it?"

CHAPTER FIVE

Morie stared up at him with wide eyes while she searched frantically for an answer that wouldn't give her away.

"The, uh, the last place I worked," she said. "The housekeeper knew all that stuff and the boss didn't like to hire staff, so I had to learn how to do those things to help her out."

"I see."

"It's just something I picked up, and, honestly, I'd rather feed calves than work in the kitchen," she added. "Just in case you had in mind to ask me to work with Mavie instead of out here."

"I didn't have that in mind."

She nodded. "Good."

He shoved his hands into the pockets of his jeans. "You don't like Gelly."

"It's not my place to like or dislike one of your friends, boss," she replied in a subdued tone. "I'm just the newest hire . . . that's all I am."

"Gelly feels threatened by you, God knows why," he added unconsciously. She might have been pretty if she did something to her hair and wore makeup and nice clothing. But she was scruffy and not very attractive most of the time. It still shook him that he'd kissed her and enjoyed it so much. He tried not to revisit that episode.

"Not my problem," she murmured, and hoped she didn't sound insolent.

"She said that the judge seemed to know you."

"Can't imagine why," she said, looking up innocently. "I sure don't travel in those circles. He might have seen me in the kitchen where I used to work, though."

"Where was that?" he asked. "The place you used to work?"

She stared at him blankly. She'd made up the name of the place, although she'd given the phone number of a friend's housekeeper who'd promised to sound convincing if anybody checked her out.

"Well?" he persisted.

She was flushed and the soy calf formula was leaking out of the oversize bottle she was using to feed him. Just when it seemed as if she was going to blow her own cover, a sudden loud noise came from outside the barn. It was followed by a barrage of range language that was even worse than what Morie had heard come out of her father during roundup.

Mallory rushed out. Morie, curious, put the calf back in his stall, set the empty bottle on a nearby shelf and followed.

Cane was throwing things. A saddle was lying on the ground. In the distance, a horse was galloping away.

"Mud-brained, unshod son of a . . . !" he raged, until he spotted Morie and bit down hard on the last word.

"What in the world is the matter with you?" Mallory asked.

Cane glared at him. His thick, short black hair was in disorder all over his head. His dark brown eyes, large and cold, were glittery with bad temper. His sensuous mouth was pulled tight against his teeth.

"I was trying to put a saddle on Old Bill," he muttered. "I thought I could manage him. I haven't been on a horse since I came home. The damned outlaw knocked me down on the saddle and ran off."

The empty sleeve, pinned at the elbow where his arm had been amputated, was poignant. Cane was ultra-sensitive about his injury. He never spoke of the circumstances under which he'd lost part of his arm, or about his military service. He drank, a lot, and kept to himself. He was avoided by most of the men, especially when he was turning the air blue, like now.

Morie sighed and went to the barn. She brought out one of the other older saddle horses they kept for visitors. This one was quite gentle, like the one that had run away. She heard Mallory telling one of the men to go after it.

She picked up Cane's saddle, ignoring his outraged, indignant look. She turned the horse and draped the saddle over his back, pulling up the cinch and fastening it deftly.

"Don't fuss," she told Cane when she handed him the bridle. "Everybody needs a little help now and then. It's not demeaning to let someone do you a favor. Even the hired help."

He glared down at her for a few seconds, during which she thought he was probably going to storm away or dress her down for her insolence.

But finally he just shook his head. "Okay. Thanks."

"You're welcome." She handed him the reins.

He was looking at the horse dubiously. It was obvious that he hadn't tried to mount one since he was wounded.

"We have a friend back in Texas that we used to go riding with," she said, without giving away much. "He lost an arm doing merc work overseas. He mounted offside so that he could use his good hand on the pommel to spring up into the saddle. Worked like a charm."

His dark eyebrows went up under the wide brim of his hat. "You don't let anybody intimidate you, do you?"

She smiled. "You're not intimidating. You're just a little scary sometimes."

He shook his head again. "Okay, I'll try it. But if I land on my face, you're fired."

"You can't fire her," Mallory pointed out. "Unless you hired her, and you didn't. Get on that horse and let's go search out straggling heifers. They really are right about snow this time."

Cane looked at his brother. "I'll give it a shot."

He fumbled the first time and almost fell. But he tried again, and again, until he got the rhythm just right. He sprang up into the saddle with a heavy sigh and took the reins in his hand. He wheeled the horse around and looked down at Morie. "Thanks."

She gave him an encouraging look. "You're welcome."

Mallory rode in between them. "Let's go. Daylight's burning."

"I'm right behind you."

Mallory glanced at Morie and he wasn't smiling. He didn't like Cane smiling at her. He didn't know why, and that made him even angrier.

"Get back to work," he told her. He rode off behind his brother without another word.

Morie glared after him. "I was going to," she muttered. "What did you think, I had a date to go sailing on the Caribbean or something?"

"Talking to yourself," Darby teased. "Better watch that. They'll be sending men with nets after you."

"If they do, I'll tell them the boss drove me batty," she assured him.

"Nice, what you did for Cane," he said, sobering. "He hasn't tried to get on a horse since he came back. I thought he'd give up after Old Bill ran off. None of us would have dared to do what you did. Saw him punch a cowboy once for even offering, a few months ago."

"He's just hurting," she said. "He

doesn't know how to cope, how to interact with people, how to go on doing normal things. I heard that he won't go to physical therapy or even talk to a psychologist. That's hurting him, too. It must be horrible, for a man so active and vital, to lose an arm."

"He was the rodeo champ," he replied solemnly. "Killed him when he had to stop competing."

"He'll adjust," she said softly. "It will take time, and help. Once he realizes that, and starts going back to the therapist, he'll learn to live with it. Like our friend did."

His eyes narrowed. "Odd friend. A mercenary."

"We have friends of all sorts." She laughed. "My dad likes renegades and odd people."

"Well, I suppose it takes all kinds to run the world," he replied. His eyes sparkled. "And we had better get back to work. Bad time to lose a job, in this economy."

"Tell me about it!"

* * *

When Cane and the boss came back, she was riding out to check the fence line.

"You keep that music box in your pocket and those earphones out of your ears while you're out alone, got that?" Mallory ordered abruptly.

She knew without asking that Tank had told him how he found her moving the broken tree limb. She grimaced. "Okay, boss."

"What sort of music do you like?" Cane asked conversationally.

"Every sort," she said with a grin. "Right now my favorite is the soundtrack from *August Rush.*"

His eyebrows arched. "Nice. Tank loves it, too. He bought the score. He's still trying to master it."

"Dalton plays?" she blurted out. She flushed and laughed when Mallory stared at her. "I noticed the grand piano in the living room. I wondered who played it."

"Tank's good," Cane said, smiling. He nodded toward Mallory. "He plays, too. Of course, he's mostly tone-deaf, but that doesn't stop him from trying."

"I can play better than Tank," Mallory said, insulted.

"Not to hear him tell it," Cane observed.

"We got the fence fixed," Mallory told her. His eyes narrowed. "You should never have tried to move that limb by yourself." He was looking pointedly at the scratch on her cheek.

She touched it self-consciously. "It only grazed me. I heal quickly."

"Even I would have called somebody to help me," Mallory persisted.

Her eyebrows arched. "Aren't you the same man who tried to lift the front end of a parked car to move it when it was blocking the barn?" she asked with a bland smile.

He glared down at her. "I would usually have called somebody to help me. I'm the boss. You don't question what I do . . . you just do what I say."

"Oh, yes, sir," she replied.

"And stop giggling," he muttered.

Her eyebrows arched. "I wasn't!"

"You were, inside, where you thought I couldn't hear it. But I can hear it."

She pursed her lips. "Okay."

He shook his head. "Let's go," he told his brother.

But Cane didn't follow. He was still looking at Morie with eyes that saw more than Mallory's did. "You know, you look very familiar to me," he said, frowning slightly. "I think I've seen you before, somewhere."

She'd had that very same feeling when she first met Cane. But she didn't remember him from any of her father's gatherings. However, he might have been with one of the cattlemen's groups that frequently toured Skylance to view King Brannt's exquisite Santa Gerts. She wasn't sure. It made her nervous. She didn't want Cane to remember where he'd seen her, if he had.

"I just have that kind of face, I expect," she said, assuming an innocent expression. "They say we all have a counterpart somewhere, someone who looks just like us."

"That might be true." He paused for a moment. "What you did—getting the horse saddled for me—that was kind. I'm sorry I was so harsh."

"It was nothing. Besides, I'm used to

harsh. I work for him." She pointed toward Mallory.

"One more word and you're a memory," Mallory retorted, but his lips twitched upward at the corners.

She laughed and went back to work.

That night, they had a series of old movies on one of the classic channels, starring Morie's grandmother, Maria Kane. It was fascinating to watch her work, to see flashes of Shelby Kane and even herself in that beautiful, elfin face and exquisite posture.

"I wish I'd known you," she whispered to the television screen. But Maria had died even before Shelby married Kingston Brannt. In fact, her funeral had been the catalyst that convinced King he couldn't live without Shelby.

Morie had heard all about her parents' romance. King and Shelby had been enemies from their earliest acquaintance. She and his brother, Danny, had been good friends who went out together on a strictly platonic basis. Then Danny had asked Shelby to pretend to be engaged to him, and he'd taken her home to Skylance. King had been eloquent in his antagonism to the match. It had provoked him into truly indefensible treatment of Shelby, for which he was later very sorry. Shelby, remembering, said that King had treated her like a princess from the day they married, trying to make up to her for all his former harsh treatment and rough words. He'd changed so much that Shelby often wondered if he was the same man she'd known in the beginning, she told her daughter.

"I can't picture Dad being mean to you." Morie had laughed. "He brings you flowers and chocolates all the time, buys you something every time he goes out of town, lavishes you with beautiful jewelry, takes you to Paris shopping. . . ."

"Yes, he's the most wonderful husband any woman could ask for, now," Shelby had replied, smiling. "But you didn't know him before." She shook her head. "It was a very difficult courtship. He was hurt by another relationship and he took it out on me." She sighed, smiling at some secret memory. "I was

showing a Western collection in New
York during Fashion Week when he
turned up in the audience. He picked
me up and carried me out of the building. I was kicking and protesting, but
he never missed a step."

Morie burst out laughing. "I can imagine Dad doing something like that," she
remarked.

Shelby sighed, her eyes dreamy. "We
had coffee and a misunderstanding. He
took me back to my apartment, prepared to say goodbye for good."

"Then what happened?" Morie asked,
fascinated by the fact that her parents
had once been young like her. It was
hard to think of them as a dating couple.

"I asked him to kiss me goodbye,"
she continued, and actually flushed.
"We got engaged in the car and we
were married three long days later."
She shook her head. "You never really
know somebody until you live with
them, Morie," she added gently. "Your
father always seemed to be the hard-
est, angriest, most untamable man on
earth. But when we were alone . . ."

She cleared her throat. The flush grew as she recalled their tempestuous, passionate wedding night and the unbelievable pleasure that had kept them in the hotel room for two days and nights with only bottled water and candy bars to sustain them through a marathon of lovemaking that had produced their first child, Cort. They were so hungry for each other that precautions had never entered their minds. But they'd both wanted children very much, so it hadn't been a problem. The memory was so poignant that it could still turn her face red.

Morie laughed. "Mom, you're blushing."

Shelby chuckled self-consciously. "Yes, well, your father is a class of his own in some ways, and I won't discuss it. It's too personal. I just hope that you're half as lucky as I've been in your choice of husbands."

Morie grimaced. "If I don't get out of here, I'll never get married. Everybody wants me because I've got a rich father."

"Some man will want you just for

yourself. The traveling accountant was a bad choice. You were vulnerable and he was a predator," Shelby said with a flash of anger. "He was very lucky that he got out of town before your father could get to him."

"I'll say." She studied Shelby. "Why won't Dad let me work on the ranch like Cort?"

"He and his father are very similar in some ways," she replied. "Jim Brannt raised him to have a great respect for women and to understand that they are much too delicate for physical labor." She shook her head. "I suppose some of that is my fault, too. You know, I lived with my aunt, and she was much the same. She didn't want me to lift a finger because ladies didn't do that. On the other hand, she hated my mother. She didn't want me to turn out like her, either."

"They play some of Grandmother's movies on television," she said. "She really was a wonderful actress. They said she married four men."

Shelby nodded. "The last was the

best . . . Brad. He died in a car crash just after I married King."

"Did Grandmother commit suicide or was that just malicious gossip?" she wondered aloud.

"I never knew," Shelby confided. "Brad said she overdosed because the studio fired her. But my aunt had often said she wasn't the suicidal kind at all. Maybe she just accidentally took too many pills to help her sleep. I'd like to believe that's the case."

"Perhaps it was."

Shelby had hugged her. "Anyway, you don't want to go around covered in mud and calf poop, really, do you?" she teased. "Even if you were muddy from archaeology, at least it was clean dirt."

Morie had burst out laughing.

Her father had come into the room during the conversation. He wore a satisfied expression as he bent to kiss Shelby and hug her close.

"I got tickets," he told her.

"To *The Firebird*?" Shelby exclaimed excitedly. "But they were sold out!"

"Old Doc Caldwell was persuaded to part with his. I thought his wife was going to kiss me to death since she hates Stravinsky," he said, and produced the tickets out of his shirt pocket. He handed them to Shelby.

"When are we going?" she asked.

"Tonight." He glanced at Morie and patted her cheek affectionately. "Sorry, kid, I couldn't get an extra ticket."

"Not a problem, Dad," she'd replied with a smile. "Debussy is more to my taste. Stravinsky is a little too experimental for my tastes."

"Want a new dress to wear to it?" King asked Shelby. "We can fly up to Dallas to Neiman Marcus."

"I have a wonderful new dress in the closet that I've been saving." She pressed close to him and was enfolded hungrily in his arms. "Thanks, sweetheart."

He kissed her hair. "Nothing's too good for my best girl."

Watching them, Morie was suddenly aware that their love for each other had only intensified since they'd been married. They were still like newlyweds, often lost in each other and unaware of anything around them. She'd hoped for that sort of romance in her own life, and she'd never found it. Cort, too, remarked that their parents were exceptionally suited to each other and that he envied that relationship.

Cort, of course, was sweet on the daughter of King's neighbor and friend, Cole Everett, who had a son and a daughter and lived nearby on the Big Spur Ranch. They frequently traded seed bulls and went to conventions together. Odalie Everett was blonde and blue-eyed like her beautiful mother, and although she wasn't really pretty, she had a voice that was soulful and clear as a bell. She sounded just like her mother, except that Heather had been a famous contemporary singer before she married her stepbrother, Cole, and Odalie was being groomed for an operatic career. Her parents were dead set against her forming any sort of relationship with a man because of her musical aspirations. It would be difficult for her to pursue such a demanding career and have a family. She had a voice that had been hailed by critics from California to New York and she was training at the Met already. Cort, unsurprisingly, had never made his feelings for her known. In fact, he pretended that he had none. He'd been Odalie's enemy for years, for reasons that no one understood. Least of all poor Odalie, who adored him.

Morie snapped back to the present. She had her own worries. Her brother would have to find his way to love all by himself. She turned her attention back to the television as the commercial ended and her grandmother came back onto the screen, larger than life.

After the movie ended, Morie looked in the mirror and was surprised to see that she was almost the image of her grandmother. If she'd used makeup and had her hair styled properly, she could have been mistaken for Maria Kane. So it was just as well that she'd neglected her hair and packed away her cosmetics to work on the Rancho Real, she decided. It would never do for people who watched old classic movies to notice that resemblance and start asking questions.

*   *   *

Darby presented her with a cell phone the next morning. "Boss said to get that for you and make sure you carry it when you're out alone. Still got that pistol I gave you in your saddlebags?"

"I do," she replied. "Have they caught that escaped killer yet?"

He shook his head. "He's a hunter. Knows these woods like the back of his hand, and is able to live off the land. It will take them a long time to hunt him down. He's got kinfolk around here, too, and the sheriff thinks some of them may be helping him hide."

"I don't know that I'd help a killer escape the law," she remarked.

"What if it was your brother or your father?" he asked simply.

She sighed. "That's a harder choice."

"Killer's got a cousin that they think might help him. They've got his place staked out. They're sure Bascomb is getting food and shelter somewhere." He shook his head. "But the cousin's place is miles from here. I don't think Joe Bascomb would turn up on the ranch."

"He doesn't have anything against

the Kirks, does he?" she asked a little worriedly.

"Not that I know of," Darby told her. "In fact, Tank testified as a character witness for him during the trial. Tank still thinks he's innocent."

"What did he do?"

"Killed a man that he said was beating up his girlfriend. Said he didn't mean to do it. He hit the man and he fell into a brick wall, hit his head and died. Would have probably been ruled accidental except the girlfriend suddenly testified that he banged the man's head against the wall and killed him deliberately."

"Why would she lie?" she asked.

"She was sweet on Bascomb, but he was in love with his late wife and didn't want anything to do with this girl. Story was, she called him to come help her because she was scared of her new boyfriend. He was fond of her, so he went. The boyfriend had hit her once or twice and Joe Bascomb intervened to save her." He sighed. "Noble effort. He saved her and he said she got even with him because he wouldn't get involved with her, although she denied it in court. It got him convicted. It's a capital offense, too. He slipped away from the transport deputy, handcuffs and leg irons and all, and hid out in the woods. They found the cuffs and irons later." He smiled. "Joe's a blacksmith. Wasn't hard for him to get free, I expect."

"He sounds like a decent man."

He nodded. "More than one decent man's gone to prison on the word of a spiteful woman, however." He checked his watch. "Best get going or you'll be late back for lunch."

"I'm on my way."

She saddled her horse and rode off.

At least she didn't have to worry about the escaped killer so much, now that she knew why he'd been convicted. Of course, he'd be desperate and she didn't want to get in his way or threaten him. But she could understand his plight. Sadly, there didn't seem to be any way to save him. He'd go to prison for life or die in the electric chair at a judge's pleasure. It didn't seem right.

She found no more breaks in the line. The weather was beautiful. The predicted snow didn't materialize. Everything was getting green and lush, and she finally took off her jacket because it was getting hot.

She paused by a stream and closed her eyes to listen to it gurgle along. She felt herself relax. A twig snapped. She whirled and looked around her, her hand tight on the bridle of her mount. A good thing, because the gelding jumped at the sound. Horses were nervous creatures, she thought, and usually with good reason. She'd seen one tear loose from a hitching post and go careening over a fence just from a pan being dropped in the kitchen.

"What is it, boy?" she asked softly, looking around with some unease.

Nothing stirred. But she cut her losses. She mounted, turned the horse and urged him into a gallop toward the ranch.

*   *   *

Later, she told Mallory about it when he came home. She found him in the kitchen drinking coffee with Mavie. He was concerned.

"It's not unlikely that Joe might come here. Tank helped him in court and thinks he's innocent," Mallory said. "But the fact is that he's an escaped, convicted killer. If you help him or Tank helps him, there will be consequences. You remember that."

"I didn't see anybody," she protested. "I just heard a branch snap, like somebody stepped on it. I thought I should tell you, just the same. Could have been an animal, I expect."

"Could have been. Or could have been Joe Bascomb," he added. "You keep your eyes open. Darby give you that cell phone?"

She nodded and produced it.

His eyes narrowed as he looked at her. "Cane said he thought he'd seen you before. Now that he mentioned it, you do look familiar."

"I told him . . . I just have that sort of face." She laughed. She couldn't react to the remark. "I might look like somebody you remember."

He frowned. "Not really. Tank and I were watching this old movie on the classics channel. It starred that actress who killed herself—what was her name? Kane," he said finally. "Maria Kane. That's it. You remind me of her."

"I do?" She smiled broadly to hide her discomfort. "Thanks! I think she was gorgeous! I watched that movie myself. I like the old black-and-white ones."

He was diverted, as she'd meant him to be. "Me, too. I'm partial to Randolph Scott and Gary Cooper and John Wayne, myself."

She raised her hand. "Bette Davis."

He made a face. "Hard as nails. I like feminine women."

She shifted uncomfortably. He was making a statement. Probably Gelly Bruner was his ideal. He'd already said he liked the pretty blonde actress in the werewolf movie. Gelly was blonde and blue-eyed, and pretty, also. Morie, with her dark hair and eyes and olive complexion, would never be to his taste. He might like kissing her, but he wasn't looking at her as if he wanted anything more from her.

"Do you ever wear anything besides slacks and shirts with writing or pictures on them?" he asked suddenly.

She stared at him. "I'd have a real hard time pulling calves in a dress." She said it with a straight face.

He gave a sudden laugh. "Damn!"

"Well, I would, boss," she said reasonably.

He just sipped his coffee. "I guess you would."

Piano music was coming from the living room. It was soft and pretty at first, then there were fumbles and then a crash. "Damn it!" Tank groaned.

They heard him get up and soon he came into the kitchen. He glanced at Morie. "I can't get the rhythm of that coda. Do you have your iPod with you, with the soundtracks on it?"

"No," she replied. She'd left it in the bunkhouse. "But I can show you."

He frowned. "You can play a piano?"

She shifted as Mallory stared openly at her. "Sort of."

"Sort of." Tank caught her hand and pulled her along with him to the living room. He seated her at the grand piano. "Show me."

CHAPTER SIX

"I just picked up a little piano playing at the last job I worked," Morie protested, denying her many years of piano lessons. "I probably can't even do an octave now."

"Can you read music?" Tank persisted.

She shifted. "Yes. A little."

"Come on, then. Play."

She couldn't figure a way out of it. They might ask all sorts of questions if they knew how well she played. She'd been offered a music scholarship in college, which she'd turned down. Her parents could well afford her tuition, and the scholarship might help some deserving student who had no such means.

After a minute's hesitation, she put her long-fingered hands on the keyboard and looked at the score before her.

She found the pedals with her foot, rested her hands on the keyboard and suddenly began to play.

Mallory, standing in the doorway, was shocked speechless. Tank, closer, smiled as he sank into an easy chair. A minute later, Cane heard the exquisite score and came into the room, as well, perching on the sofa.

Lost in the music, Morie played with utter joy. It had been weeks since she'd had access to a piano, and this one was top quality. It had been tuned recently, as well. The sounds that came from it were as exquisite as the score she was playing with such expression.

When the final, poignant crescendo was reached and she played the last notes, there was an utter stillness in the room and, then, exuberant applause.

She got up, embarrassed and flushed. "I only play a little," she protested. "Thanks."

Mallory was staring at her through narrowed eyes. "Aren't you full of surprises, for a poor cowgirl," he remarked with faint suspicion.

She bit her lower lip, hard. "All of us have natural talent of some sort. I always knew how to play. I played by ear for a long time, then this nice lady took me in and tutored me where I worked last." Actually, it had been Heather Everett, who played as well as she sang.

"And where was that, did you say?" Mallory persisted.

But this time he didn't catch her out. "The Story Ranch outside Billings." She happened to know that the ranch had been sold after the owner's death. There was nobody who could deny her story. And she could always give him the phone number of the housekeeper who'd promised to cover her allegations.

Mallory actually looked disappointed. "I see."

"He was a grand old fellow to work

for," she elaborated. "He had a piano and he let me practice on it. I was heartbroken when he died." She was certain that she would have been, if she'd known him. Her father spoke of the old gentleman with great affection. He knew him from cattlemen's conventions.

"You have a real talent," Cane remarked. "Have you thought about a career using it?"

"Shut up," Mallory said at once, glaring at his brother. "I'm not looking for a new hire to look after my prize heifers because she—" he indicated her "—wants to go off looking for a recording contract!"

"She should use her talent," Cane argued hotly. "She's wasting her life working for pennies, using up her health lifting heavy limbs off fences! Down the road, she'll pay for all this physical labor. She's too slightly built to even be doing it!"

Mallory knew that, but it irritated him that his brother had pointed it out to him. "She asked for the job and was willing to do whatever it involved!" he shot back.

Cane stood up, dark eyes glittering. "And you're taking advantage of it!"

"You could send somebody with her to ride fences," Tank interjected, stepping between the brothers. He smiled at Morie, who was looking with stifled horror at the confrontation she'd provoked so innocently. "In fact, I could ride them with her. I've got enough time free."

"Or I could," Cane said shortly. "You need to work on marketing for the production sale. I'm the one with the most free time."

"She works for me, damn it!" Mallory ground out. "I tell her what to do. You don't hire and fire! Either of you! Personnel problems are my business!"

"I am not a problem!" Morie said, and stomped her foot at the three brothers. "Listen, I don't mind doing whatever my job calls for, honest I don't. I really appreciate your kindness. But I just work here. I'm a hired hand."

They stared at her.

"Your hands are precious," Cane said

gently, and with feeling, because he only had one left and he knew better than any of the other brothers how precious they truly were. "You mustn't risk them on physical labor."

"I'll buy her a pair of damned gloves, then!" Mallory snapped. "Want me to hire a companion for her, to do the hard jobs, while I'm at it?"

Morie felt sick. She lowered her eyes and moved away. "I'll get back to work," she said in a faint tone. "I never meant to cause trouble. I'm really sorry."

She went out the door before they could stop her.

"Oh, you're a real prince," Cane shot at his older brother. "Now she's upset!"

"I should go after her," Tank agreed.

"I'll go after her," Cane replied curtly, starting for the door.

"What the hell is the matter with you two?" Mallory demanded hotly. "She's an employee! She's a hire!"

They glared at him.

"You've already forgotten Vanessa, have you?" he asked with a cold smile.

They sobered at once.

"She was handing our family heirlooms out the window to her lover, when we caught her," he reminded them. "She was sweet and caring, and the best cook in two counties. She pampered us. Brought hot chocolate and cookies out to the barn in the snow when we couldn't leave sick bulls. Made soup for us when we had to take turns staying in the line cabins, before market prices shot up. Treated us like princes. And all the while, she was pricing the stuff in the cabinets, the paintings, the silver services, the china, the crystal that was in our family for a hundred years."

They looked shamefaced.

"She came with excellent references, too," Mallory continued. "Except when I finally got around to checking them out, they were bogus. She lied even when we caught her red-handed. Her lover had made her do it. She was innocent. She loved working for us. She'd do anything if we'd forgive her and let her come back. She'd testify against her lover, even."

"But she had a record as long as my leg," Tank put in quietly.

"And a real talent for lying." Cane nodded.

"And we almost lost the ranch because she sued us for defamation of character and sexual harassment, of which we were totally innocent."

"Good thing the jury believed us," Cane replied.

"Good thing we had the best damned attorney in Wyoming," Mallory agreed. "We can't afford to trust people we don't know. Gelly is already suspicious of Morie, and she's come to me twice with stories that Morie denies and makes light of." He shifted. "I don't trust her." He didn't add that his own great physical attraction to her was one of his biggest issues. It made him vulnerable. He couldn't afford to trust his instincts, when they might be leading him down a dark road. "She knows how to make canapés and plan society dos, and play the piano like a professional. It doesn't jibe with her job description."

"Then what do you think is her real background?" Cane asked curtly.

"Think about it," Mallory replied. "A woman who wanted to insinuate herself into a rich household, without drawing attention to her background, would pretend to know nothing about wealthy people. But underneath, she'd be clued in about how they lived, what they did. She'd know their habits and their tastes. She'd have to, to play up to them. Then she'd bring out those talents, a little at a time, to deepen the mystery and make herself acceptable."

"You're reaching," Tank said shortly. "Gelly's poisoned you against Morie."

"I was already headed in that direction," Mallory replied. "She isn't telling us the truth about her background. I'm sure of it."

"That doesn't mean it's a shady background," Cane replied. "Vanessa poisoned all of us against women for a while. It's why we hired Mavie, who isn't young or beautiful or interested in us. But Morie might be the genuine article."

"And she might not be," Mallory said grimly. "I just think we need to keep an eye on her and not trust her too far. Just like any other new hire."

They had to agree. They'd gone in

headfirst, because she seemed sweet
and helpful and kind. But it could be an
act. They knew from experience how
gullible all three of them could be.

"I guess you're right," Cane said solemnly.

"I'm always right," Mallory said,
tongue-in-cheek. "I'm the eldest."

Tank glared at him. "Only by two
years. Don't get conceited."

Mallory chuckled. "Better get back
to work."

Morie was disconcerted by the argument. She was preoccupied when she
went to the tack room to get her bridle
and saddle to ride fence. There was a
lot of fence on the ranch. She'd never
seen so many acres, except on her father's spread. This was a huge tract of
land that made up the ranch property,
and it was cross-fenced for miles and
miles and miles.

Darby glanced at her as she came
out. "Trouble?" he asked gently.

She hesitated. She nodded.

"Mallory again?"

"I started a fight. I didn't mean to. I was just playing the piano."

His eyebrows arched. "That was you?" he exclaimed. "I thought it was a record they'd put on!"

She looked down shyly. "I took piano for almost ten years," she said. "I love to play. Tank, I mean Mr. Kirk, had the score from that movie, *August Rush,* and when he knew I could play, he asked me to show him. So I did. But then the brothers said I shouldn't be risking my hands doing manual labor and Mallory, I mean Mr. Kirk, got mad and said I was hired to do ranch work. . . ."

"I see where this is going," Darby replied quietly. "It must have been difficult."

She nodded again and drew in a long breath. "I didn't mean to start trouble. It was so wonderful to have a piano to play on." She smiled. "I've loved music all my life. I can play classical guitar, too, and I used to carry a guitar with me wherever I went. But you can't pack a piano around, so I sort of got out of the habit of playing." She closed her eyes. "I can hear sonatas in my mind, when I go to bed. I never met a classical score that I didn't love. Especially Debussy . . ."

"Am I paying you for musical commentary now?" Mallory asked coldly from the doorway.

She started, and almost dropped the saddle. "Sorry, boss. Sorry." She rushed out the door with the saddle over her shoulder, almost tripped and fell down the steps in her rush.

Darby put out a hand and pulled Mallory around. His blue eyes were blazing. "Lay off," he said in a menacing tone. "The girl's had enough for one day."

Mallory shook off the hand and glared at his foreman. "Don't push me."

"Then don't push her," Darby said. "Look at her, for God's sake!"

He didn't want to, but he did. She was fumbling with the saddle. Her hands were shaking. Tears were rolling down her cheeks. Mallory felt it through his heart, like a knife. He grimaced.

"If I was her, I'd quit right now," Darby said shortly. "And when she comes back tonight, that's what I'm going to advise her to do. I know a couple of ranchers who need help. . . ."

"You'll keep your mouth shut, or you'll be the one leaving," Mallory told him angrily. "Don't interfere."

"Then you stop treating her like the black plague" came the short reply. "Honest to God, what's wrong with you? I've never seen you treat a kid like that!"

"She's no kid," Mallory said angrily. "She's a woman." He knew it far better than Darby.

"Well, maybe so," he conceded. "Still, she's twice the woman that blond headache you take around with you is," he told the boss. "You're letting her warp your idea of Morie. She's making you suspicious. Now you're picking holes in everything Morie does. All because you and your brothers were taken in by Vanessa Wilkes. It's your pride, hurting and making you suspect everybody. Even poor old Harry. He never stole that drill. Your girlfriend was in the bunkhouse just before she told you she'd seen him take it. She framed him, and you let her."

"That's enough," Mallory said. He looked dangerous. "He was guilty."

"He wasn't, but he knew he'd never convince you as long as Gelly was around. Now she's trying to do the same to Morie, to make you run her off." He straightened. "I've seen good people and I've seen bad people. I warned you about Vanessa and you wouldn't listen. Now I'm telling you, Morie isn't like that. She's pure gold. If you aren't careful, you'll ruin her life. Maybe your own, too."

"She's not what she seems," Mallory said.

"Who is?" Darby smiled gently. "But she's not devious. She's running from something. I don't know what. But she had no idea how to do ranch work, I'll tell you that."

"What!"

"She was desperate for a job," Darby said. "So I taught her how to do the chores, how to dip cattle, how to help brand, how to stack hay and ride fence and pull calves. You have to admit, she's turned into one of the best hires we've ever had. Works all hours, never complains about anything." His eyes narrowed and the smile thinned. "And you think someone like that could be dishonest? Wouldn't she be complaining at every turn and trying to get out of hard work?"

"I don't know," Mallory confessed. "Vanessa made me question my judgment. I'm not certain about anyone anymore."

"If you want to distrust somebody, you take a hard look at that Bruner woman," Darby said. "Something's not right there. I'd bet money on it."

"She's just a friend," Mallory muttered.

"She doesn't think that. She wants you. And she'll find a way to get rid of Morie, you mark my words. She's not going to let her stay here."

"It's my ranch. I hire and fire."

"Think so? We'll see. Meanwhile, how about easing up on Morie?" he added. "God knows what that child's been through in her life to make her end up here, doing a job she was never intended to do. Hurts me to see that deep scratch on her face. Flawless complexion. She could have been a model."

Mallory frowned. He hadn't considered her complexion or her background. He'd only been concerned that she might be a con artist. He'd have to take a better look at her. On the one hand, he was suspicious. On the other, he trusted Darby's judgment when he couldn't trust his own.

He patted the old man on the shoulder. "Never could take back talk from anybody but you, you old pirate."

Darby grinned. "You'll always get the truth from me. Even if you don't want to hear it."

Mallory sighed. He was looking after Morie. She'd gone galloping off, still crying. He felt like a villain. "Think I'll take a ride."

Darby smiled. "Good idea. You do that."

Morie stopped at the creek and got off the horse. She bathed her face in the clean water and used her only handkerchief to mop up her tears. Ridiculous, letting that awful man make her cry. She should have kicked him and told him what he could do with his job. That's what her father would have done. He'd never have gone off crying. She tried to picture that and it made her smile.

She heard a horse coming up and turned, expecting Darby. But it was the boss. He looked oddly contrite, watching her with one arm crossed over the pommel, his dark eyes keen on her tearstained face.

"Maybe I could have chosen my words better," he said stiffly.

She shrugged and looked away. "I work here. You're the boss."

"Yes, but . . ." He drew in an angry breath. "Why didn't you fight back? Why did you run?"

She glared at him. "I've caused enough trouble for one day," she said flatly. She drew in a long breath. "Listen, I should quit. . . ."

"No!"

He was out of the saddle in a heartbeat and standing over her the next.

He took her by the shoulders. In the silence of the woods, she could hear her own heart beating as he looked into her eyes and didn't look away for so long that her heart ran wild. She had to part her full lips to breathe. Her heartbeat was strangling her.

He saw that helpless reaction and it touched him. She couldn't have faked her attraction to him. It was far too visible.

His hands relaxed and became caressing. They ran up and down her arms in the long-sleeved cotton T-shirt. "You puzzle me," he said, his voice deep and slow, like velvet. "I don't like it."

Her hands pressed against the soft cotton of his shirt. Underneath it she felt cushy, thick hair and hard muscle. She smelled the woodsy cologne and the masculine soap that clung to his skin. He made her tingle all over, just by standing close to her. She looked up at his wide, sensuous mouth and remembered how it felt to kiss him. She wanted him to kiss her. She wanted it, so much!

"Damn it," he ground out, because he knew. He could sense her hunger, even before her rapt gaze on his lips proved it to him.

Before she could question the sudden curse, his mouth went down on hers. He kissed her hungrily. His arms lifted her into the instantly hard contours of his powerful body and pulled her into him. His hand went to the base of her spine, insistent as he demonstrated the force of his desire for her.

She tried to protest, but her own body betrayed her. She moaned and pressed close against him, her mouth twisting under his, provoking, pleading, begging for more.

She felt him move, felt the ground suddenly under her back and the weight and warmth of his body melting down into hers. She felt his long leg parting both of hers as his hips moved down between them.

"Dear . . . God!" he bit off reverently as he felt the pleasure wash over him.

His hands were under her shirt, under her bra. He felt the softness of her small, firm breasts with their hard tips first against his fingers, and then, as he pushed the shirt up out of his way, under his mouth.

He suckled her, hard, feeling her arch under him and cry out. He thought he was hurting her in his ardor and started to lift his head, but her hands pulled, pleaded, dragged his mouth back down.

She tasted like honey. He was drowning in need. He pressed against her in a slow, sensuous rhythm that grew more insistent by the minute. His hand lifted her hips, pulled them against the hardness of him.

He worked feverishly at the buttons of his shirt and opened it so that he could feel her breasts under the crush of his bare chest. His mouth invaded hers. He was desperate to have her. He couldn't bear to stop, not now!

Neither could she. It was the most passionate interlude of her young life. She wasn't able to protest. She wanted to know him, as a man, as a lover. She wanted to feel him deep inside her, feel him taking her, possessing her. She wanted . . . a child . . . !

She hadn't realized she'd spoken aloud until he suddenly dragged himself away from her, rolled over in an agonized state of denial and groaned as if all the devils in purgatory were pummeling him.

She lay shocked, gasping, as she realized how far they'd gone. She jack-knifed, quickly righting her clothing, shivering with denied pleasure. She got to her feet, shaking, and looked away while she fought to get her breath. She was horrified at her own lack of control. It had been so close!

She swallowed, hard, and then swallowed again. She couldn't force herself to look at him, although she heard him get to his feet, heard his own rasping breath as he worked to regain the control he'd lost.

After a minute, she heard a rough curse break from his throat as he looked at her stiff back.

"So that's your game, is it?" he asked coldly. "You'd like a child, would you? I don't suppose you're taking any sort of preventative. You seduce the boss, there's a child and you're set for life. That how it works?"

She turned, shocked. She stared at him with stark embarrassment and averted her eyes. She was flushed and sick at heart. "I . . . wasn't thinking at all."

"Obviously you were," he said coldly. He smiled. It wasn't a nice smile. "Good try. But I'm no novice with your sex, and I'm no easy mark."

"It wasn't like that." She faltered, flushing even more.

He gave her a long and very insulting look. "Sure." He picked up his hat from where he'd tossed it, dusted it off, slanted it over his eyes and went to find his horse, which had wandered off to eat green grass. He mounted and turned the horse. He stared at her, but she didn't look at him, or answer him. She went to get back on her own mount and rode away without another word.

She was going to have to leave. She knew it certainly. Mallory had made his opinion of her quite clear. What was unclear was why he'd suddenly started kissing her like that. She hadn't asked for it. Or had she? Her obvious attraction to him was going to be disastrous. He was already suspicious of her, thanks to his girlfriend. She'd blurted out that embarrassing comment and now he was surely going to think she was some gold digger.

Her subconscious must be working overtime, she decided, because she had no conscious thought of starting a family. But to have a child, with a man like Mallory, who was so masculine and attractive . . .

And bullheaded and suspicious-minded and unkind, she added hotly to herself. Of course she wanted a child from a man like that!

Actually, in her young life, she'd never known passion or such hunger; she'd never thought of marrying and having children. She'd thought herself in love with the persistent accountant until she found out his true motives for courting her. But now she knew there had been nothing at all to that relationship. And he'd pressed her to sleep with him. He'd even said they had no need for birth control, because he wanted children with her. Somehow, she'd had the sense to deny him.

Mallory was thinking the exact same thing about her that she'd thought about her would-be lover. The accountant, she still couldn't bring herself to say his name even silently, had wanted to trap her into marriage. Mallory thought Morie was up to the same underhanded game. It was humiliating.

She should have had more control of herself. It was just that he was heaven to kiss. And kissing had so quickly not been enough to satisfy either of them. If she hadn't opened her mouth to say something so shocking, if he hadn't pulled back in time . . .

She flushed, remembering how sweet it had been. She couldn't allow that to happen again. Not that she'd be around long enough. She'd started trouble with the brothers, innocently, setting one against the other. Her presence here was causing problems. She should leave. Now. Today.

Yes. She should. She got back on her horse and started to turn him toward the ranch. But at the last minute, she couldn't force herself to do it. Just a little longer, she promised herself. Just a few more days to look at Mallory from a distance and talk to him and dream of him. What would it hurt?

She started back to the fence line.

Several days passed with no other incidents. Mallory, however, said hardly two words to Morie. He relayed instructions through Darby, who seemed uncomfortable for some reason.

Cane found Morie at the line cabin, where she was spending the day watching for calves to drop. He got off his horse with some little effort and walked up on the porch. Morie was drinking coffee from her thermos and eating a cold, buttered biscuit.

"Hi," she greeted cheerily. "Want to share lunch?" She held out the half-eaten biscuit.

He shook his head. "No, thanks. I just had a thick roast-beef sandwich with homemade French fries."

She groaned and looked at the biscuit. "I knew I wasn't living right."

He smiled. He pushed his wide-brimmed hat back on his head and his dark eyes narrowed. "What's going on between you and Mal?" he asked unexpectedly.

She fumbled and spilled coffee on her jeans. Well, they were dirty anyway. "What . . . what do you mean?" She faltered, and ruined her poise by flushing.

He pursed his lips. "I see."

"No, you don't," she shot back. "You don't see. There's nothing. Nothing at all!"

"Why, because he's the boss and you're the hired help?" he asked, leaning back against a post. "We aren't royalty."

"You might as well be," she said flatly. "He thinks I'm after his money."

His eyebrows arched. "He does?"

She lowered her eyes to the splash of coffee on her knee. She sipped more coffee. "I'm not," she said with quiet pride, "but it's what he thinks." She looked up. "I'm fairly certain his girlfriend is helping him to think it. She really hates my guts."

"I noticed."

She looked up at him solemnly. "You watch her," she said with sudden passion. "She's pretending to be something she's not."

His eyebrows arched. "And you know this, how . . . ?"

"For one thing, she's wearing last year's colors. For another, the shoes she favors are far out of style. Her jewelry is just as dated, and the purse she carries is couture, but it's not a new one."

His eyebrows arched more. "Excuse me?"

She shifted restlessly and averted her eyes. "I have a friend who models," she lied. It was her mother, who was her closest friend. "I know what's in style and what's not, something Ms. Bruner seems unaware of. I suppose she thinks men don't follow fashion and wouldn't know." She met his gaze. "She's trying to pose as a socialite, but something's not right about her. Want some advice? Get a private detective to do just a surface check of her back-

ground. I'm betting you'd find something interesting."

"Why don't you tell Mal?" he asked.

She laughed coldly. "Oh, sure, he'd
listen to me. He already thinks I'm a
gold-digging opportunist."

He sighed. "You're not what you're
pretending to be, either, are you?"

She smiled wryly. "No," she confessed. "But I'm an honest person. I'm
not hiding from the law or contemplat-
ing breaking it. Actually, I have a cousin
who's a Texas Ranger. I've known him
and looked up to him since I was able
to walk. He'd disown me if I did anything criminal. So would my parents."

"Why are you working here?"

"You'd be surprised," she assured
him.

"I might be, at that." He hesitated.
"Want me to go ride fence with you?
I've got some free time. That killer is
still on the loose." He sobered. "I
wouldn't want anything to happen to
you."

She was pleasantly surprised at his
protective attitude. "Thanks," she said
and meant it. "But I'm fine. I've got the

cell phone the boss was kind enough to provide, and I've got a gun that Darby loaned me. I'll be fine."

He regarded her quizzically. "Okay, then. I'll leave you to it. A cold biscuit. You call that lunch?"

She sighed. "It's a lovely biscuit. Mavie made them for me."

"She's a super cook."

"Yes, she is. Thanks again," she added as he mounted his horse and started to ride off.

"You're welcome."

He tipped his hat and rode away. Morie finished her biscuit and coffee and went back to work.

CHAPTER SEVEN

Morie was confused about her feelings for Mallory and her growing concern about Gelly Bruner's interference and antagonism. The woman really hated her, and she was going to find a way to make trouble. Not that Morie was willing to run from a fight. If worse came to worst, she could always tell them the truth about herself. Except that Mallory, who hated lies, would think her a hopeless liar and probably never speak to her again.

She finished her cold biscuit and cooling coffee and sighed. Just as she started to get up, she heard a twig snap. There was another sound of movement, rhythmic. Any hunter knew that to walk normally was a dead give-away to prey he was stalking. Animals never moved rhythmically. They'd hear the odd rhythm and know it was a hu-man even before they caught his scent.

Morie looked toward her saddled horse, where her pistol was. She did have her cell phone in her pocket, though. She stood up and pulled it out, fumbling as she tried to turn it on. Of all the times not to have it activated . . . !

"Don't do that" came a curt, mascu-line command from behind her.

She whirled, frightened and shocked, to see a tall, sandy-haired man with a hunting rifle standing just a few yards away. She trembled and dropped the phone. Her wide brown eyes were ap-palled as she looked at the rifle and hoped that she'd lived a good enough life that she wouldn't go somewhere horrible when she died.

She didn't speak. It would be use-less. Either he'd kill her or he wouldn't. But the bore of that rifle barrel looked ten inches wide as she stared down it. She lifted her hands and waited.

But surprisingly, he didn't shoot. He lowered the gun. "Where did Tank go?" he asked suddenly.

"T . . . tank?"

"Tank Kirk," he said curtly. His blue eyes were dark and glittery.

"That wasn't Tank. It was Cane." She faltered. "He just came to offer to ride the fence line with me, because there's an escaped murderer on the loose."

"Murderer," he scoffed. "It was an accident. The idiot fell into a brick wall and his even more idiotic girlfriend lied and said I did it deliberately. Getting even, because I knew what she was and I wanted no part of her."

She lowered her hands slowly. Her heart was slamming against her ribs. "You're Joe Bascomb." She faltered.

"Yes, unfortunately." He sighed. He stared at her. "Have you got anything to eat out here? I'm so sick of rabbit and squirrel—bad time of year to eat either. They're not really in season. But a man gets hungry."

"I have a biscuit left. No coffee, I'm

sorry, but I have a bottle of water." She offered both.

He put down the rifle and ate the biscuit with odd delight, closing his eyes on the taste. "Mavie must have made these." He sighed. "Nobody cooks like she does." He finished it off in a heartbeat and washed it down with half the bottle of water.

Morie watched him with open curiosity. He didn't act like a murderer.

He noted her gaze and laughed shortly. "I wasn't going to end up in a maximum-security prison while my lawyer spins out appeal after appeal. I hate cages. God, I hate cages! To think I could ever end up like this because of some spiteful, vicious woman . . . !"

"If you'd had a good defense attorney, he could have taken her apart on the witness stand," she returned.

"My attorney is from legal aid, and they come in all sizes. This one's meek and mild and thinks that women have been victimized too much in courts, so she wouldn't say anything to hurt my accuser's feelings."

"You should have asked the judge to appoint someone else."

"I did. They couldn't get anyone else to volunteer." He sighed heavily and ran a restless big hand through his hair. "She did say she'd appeal. I think she finally realized that I was innocent, after I'd been convicted. She said she was sorry." He glared at Morie. "Sorry! I'm going to get the needle, and she's sorry!"

"So am I," she said gently. "The justice system usually works. But people are the odd element in any trial. Mistakes get made."

"You'd know this, how?" he asked, but with a smile.

"My uncle is a state supreme court judge," she replied. "In Texas."

His eyebrows arched. "Impressive."

She smiled. "Yes, it is. He used to work for legal aid and donate time, when he was younger. He still believes everyone is entitled to proper representation."

"I wish he sat on the bench in Wyoming," Bascomb replied sadly.

"You should turn yourself back in,"

she advised. "This is only going to make things worse for you."

"They couldn't get much worse," he replied. "I lost my wife last year. She died of a heart attack. She was only twenty-nine years old. Who dies of a heart attack at twenty-nine?" he exclaimed.

"There was a football player at my high school who dropped dead on the playing field at age seventeen of an unknown heart problem," Morie replied. "He was a sweet boy. We all mourned him. People get all sorts of disorders at young ages. You don't think of little children having arthritis, either, do you? But some grammar-school kids have rheumatoid arthritis that limits them in all sorts of ways. Kids also have diseases like diabetes. We don't only get things wrong with us when we're old."

"I guess so. It's not a perfect world, is it?" he added.

She shook her head.

He finished the bottle of water. "Thanks. I've been going by my mom's place for food, but they've got people watching it. I don't want her to suffer for what I've done. I've been hunting for food."

"What about water?" she asked gently. "It's dangerous to drink water from springs. . . ."

He pulled a packet of tablets out of his vest pocket and showed her. "It makes any water potable," he said. "I was in the military. Tank and I served together in Iraq. That seems like a hundred years ago." He grimaced. "He testified for me. It was a real brave thing to do, when everybody thought I was guilty. The local boy's family is known and loved, and that made it a lot harder for me to get an unbiased jury. In fact—" he sighed "—one of the jurors was actually an illegitimate blood relation. My attorney didn't catch that on voir dire, either."

She caught her breath. "That's a disqualification. Grounds for a retrial."

"You think so?" he asked, curious.

"I do. You should speak to your attorney."

He laughed shortly. "She's not my attorney anymore. I read in a discarded newspaper that she said she couldn't represent someone who proved himself guilty by running away. So now I've got no defense and nobody to advise me."

She moved a step closer. "I'm advising you. Turn yourself in before it's too late."

He shook his head. "Can't do that. I can't survive locked up in a cage. I've had months of it. I'd rather die than go back, and that's the truth."

She could sympathize. She didn't like closed places, either. "It will go harder on you that you didn't wait for an appeal."

"I don't care," he said heavily. "My wife is dead . . . the life I had is all gone. I've got no reason to go on anyway. If they shoot me down in the woods, well, it won't be so bad. God forgives people. Even bad people. I don't think He'll send me to purgatory."

"You can't give up," she said, driven to comfort him. "God puts us here for a reason. We may never know why. It may be to inspire one person, or give another a reason to keep them from suicide, or be in the right place to give aid to save someone's life who may one day save the world. Who knows? But I believe we have a purpose. All of us."

"And what do you think mine is?" he asked with amusement. She was so fervent in her beliefs.

"I don't know," she replied. "But you have a part to play. I'm sure of that. Don't give up. Don't ever give up."

"There was this movie *Galaxy Quest* with Tim Allen and Alan Rickman, kind of a *Star Trek* spoof," he recalled. "Their running line was 'Never give up, never surrender!'"

"I saw that one. It was terrific," she replied, smiling.

He shrugged. "I guess it wasn't such a bad credo, at that." He shouldered the gun. "Don't tell anybody I was here," he said.

She bit her lower lip. It sounded like a threat.

He gave her a long-suffering look. "You might get in trouble for giving me food and water," he added.

She relaxed. "Oh. Thanks."

"I'm a wanted man," he replied quietly. "I'm not giving up, no matter what. They'll have to take me down. Prison is a horrible place for an outdoorsman." He looked around at the towering trees and the blue, blue sky. "This is my cathedral," he said solemnly. "There's no place closer to God than the forest." He drew in the scent of it with closed eyes. "I should never have let her talk me into going to her apartment," he said. "She was screaming. She said her boyfriend was banging on the door threatening to kill her and I was the only person she knew that she could trust to deal with him. I must have been out of my mind," he added remorsefully. "She was fending him off when I got there, but he muttered something about her attacking him first. She set us both up. I don't think she meant for him to die, or me to go to prison . . . It was just a misguided plea for attention. But she caused it. Now she's the injured party and I'm being sued for wrongful death by his family." He gave her a long look.

She winced. "I'm sorry."

"Hell, so am I," he said heavily. "Don't know what I ever did to deserve this."

"It's a trial," she replied. "All of us have them. It's part of the process of life. You'll get through it," she added firmly.

"Think so? If I were a gambler, I'd take that bet and get rich on it." He looked at her clothing and laughed. "Well, maybe not. You don't look any better off than I was, no offense."

"None taken," she replied.

"I have to go. Thanks for the help. But if I'm caught, I'll swear you never did a thing to help me," he added.

"And I'll swear that I did," she said proudly. "I'm not afraid of due process. My uncle is a judge. He'd find someone good to represent me."

His blue eyes smiled at her. "Lucky you. Thanks, kid."

She laughed. "You're welcome. I wish I could help you."

His face softened. "You're a nice person. My wife was like that. She'd have helped anybody, in the law or out of it. I miss her so much."

"It's just a little separation," she said.

"We all go, eventually. It's a matter of time."

He cocked his head. "She'd have said that, too." He looked around. "You be careful out here, all alone. It's dangerous sometimes. There are other people who shun society. Some of them are homeless people with various mental disturbances. They could hurt you."

"I know. I've got a phone."

"Keep it on," he advised drily.

"Yes, well if I'd had it on, the police would already be here, wouldn't they?" she said pointedly.

He chuckled. "I guess so." He gave her a last look. "Be safe."

"You, too."

He turned and walked back into the woods. She noted that when he was almost out of sight, the rhythm of his footsteps changed and became halting and unsteady. Like an animal's gait. She realized then that he'd walked in a human pattern to alert her to his presence, so that he wouldn't frighten her too much by appearing suddenly. She felt sorry for him. She wondered if she

could get in touch with Uncle Danny
and find him some help. Even if he was
guilty as sin, he needed a lawyer. Uncle
Danny would know someone. She was
certain of it.

That night, she called him. She knew
his habits quite well, and one of them
was to work very late at his office on
nights when circuit court was in ses-
sion. Sure enough, he answered the
phone himself. He was surprised but
pleased to hear from her.

"Having fun at your job?" he asked,
amused that she'd defied King to work
as a cowgirl on a ranch.

"Lots," she replied. "But I miss you."

"I miss you, too, sweetie," he replied.
"Not prying, but is there some reason
besides love that you're calling me at
night? Got a problem?"

"Sort of," she said. "There's this escaped convict who was framed . . ."

"Oh, spare me," he said heavily.
"Honey, you have no idea how many
innocent people are serving life terms
in federal prison. They were framed,

the cops were dishonest, somebody was getting even with them . . ."

"But it's not like that." She faltered. "Tank Kirk was a character witness for him. The man fought in Iraq. His wife died. This other woman chased him and couldn't get him, so she set him up by crying for help when her boy-friend was beating her up. The guy came to her rescue, struggled with the man, who hit his head and died. The woman then swore that the convict did it deliberately. It's her word against his, and he only had a public defender."

"Careful, darlin', I was a public de-fender," he chided. "It's a noble call-ing."

"Yes, well this public defender was on the woman's side and wouldn't press the case. There's something else. There was a blood relative of the victim on the jury and it wasn't caught in voir dire."

"Now that's another matter, a very serious one," Danny replied. "His attor-ney should press for a retrial on that basis, if she can prove it."

"He isn't represented," she replied.

"His attorney quit when he escaped and ran from the law."

"Oh, boy."

"I know. I shouldn't get involved. But he seems a decent man. You'd have to know the Kirk brothers to understand why I think he's innocent. Tank isn't easily fooled about people."

"Ah. But he's fooled about you, isn't he?"

She had to concede that point. "Touché."

"Tell you what. I know some people in the judiciary in Wyoming. I'll make a few phone calls. What's the man's name?"

"Joe Bascomb."

"Okay. But you stay out of it. Believe me, you don't want to be charged as an accessory, in aiding an escaped convict," he added.

"Yes, I know. I won't. Thanks."

"Hey, how could I turn down my favorite girl?" he teased. "See you soon. Take care."

"You, too."

She closed up the little phone with a sigh. It wasn't any of her business. But the man had seemed so personable. He could have killed her, attacked her, if he'd wanted to. There had been nobody to help her. But he'd been polite and courteous and kind. It spoke volumes about the sort of person he was. She had to help if she could. And you never knew, she considered. There was a pattern to life. He'd become entwined in hers. There had to be a reason, somewhere. She might find it out one day.

The next morning, Mallory was looking at her with more suspicion than ever. She walked over to him, trying not to notice how very attractive he was. She wished she could have met him in her real persona, as she was, so that things would have been on an equal footing from the beginning. As it was, he'd know someday that she'd lied to him about her status. Or perhaps he wouldn't. She could go home, go back to the old life, marry the nice clean-cut young millionaire her father was pressing her to marry and settle down. She could forget the rough rancher who lived in Wyoming and thought she was shady and untrustworthy. If only he could know how much those accusations hurt her.

She looked up at him with wide dark eyes. "Something wrong, boss?"

"You know that we keep a record of all outgoing phone calls here?" he asked solemnly.

Her heart jumped. She'd called Texas. In fact, she'd called her uncle's office.

"Do you?" she asked, trying to sound innocent.

"I'd like to know why you were phoning a superior court judge in Texas," he said simply. He shoved his hands into his pockets and gave her a cold smile. "In fact, the same superior court judge who flew up here for our party. Did you discuss something more than canapés when you met him outside and Gelly caught you? Is he your lover? Or do you have a lawsuit in mind and you're looking for advice? I do recall that you threatened to sue Gelly."

Her heart raced while she searched for excuses that wouldn't sound any more alarm bells. She didn't want to

DIANA PALMER   201

give away Tank's friend. If Mallory knew she'd seen the man in the woods, he might call the sheriff. She didn't want to cause the poor man any more trouble than she already had.

"I forgot to add something to the recipe I gave him," she blurted out.

He blinked and stared at her. "Excuse me?"

"The canapé recipe," she continued. "I forgot to tell him how long his housekeeper should cook them. He said they were having some big to-do on his family's ranch next month and he wanted the recipe for that."

"So you called him in the middle of the night to tell him?" he asked, incredulous.

She grimaced. "It was when I remembered it," she replied, and shrugged. "I forget stuff."

"Not his phone number, apparently," he mused.

"It was listed on the internet," she muttered, prevaricating because it was for a good cause. "I used a search engine. I knew his name and what he did for a living. The rest was easy."

He let out a long breath. He always seemed to be suspicious of her, and he hated himself for it. She seemed to be an honest, hardworking, kind young woman. But he didn't trust his instincts. He'd been taken in one time too many by a woman who wasn't what she seemed. This one knew her way around the law, despite her protests, and she could pose a real threat to the ranch if she was trying to set him up.

On the other hand, his heart started doing cartwheels every time he looked at her, and that was getting worse by the day. He wanted her. He was having a hard time hiding it, especially from his brothers, who noticed everything.

Gelly was furious that he even talked about Morie, which he did often, involuntarily. He'd mentioned her help in the kitchen, which Mavie had been overjoyed to have. Gelly wouldn't dirty her fingers in a kitchen, and she was already jealous. Too jealous. He'd let the woman get too familiar with him, just by not pushing her away when he still could. Now she was talking about marriage and interceding with him for a friend who wanted to buy some scrubland on the northernmost end of the ranch.

"It's just worthless land," she coaxed. "You can't run cattle on it. This poor man just lost everything he had. He just wants a few acres to live on. Maybe grow a little garden."

"If it's land you can't run cattle on, you sure as hell can't farm it, Gelly," he'd replied. "Besides, it's a family ranch and that would be a family decision. You need to have the man come and talk to us."

She didn't dare do that. The brothers would realize in a heartbeat that he was a businessman, not a down-on-his-luck rancher.

"Oh, he's out of town," she said, thinking quickly.

"Doing what?"

She thought. "Visiting his sick brother."

He shrugged. "No problem. Have him come see us when he gets back. Now, are you hell-bent on going to this movie?" he added, indicating it on the screen of his computer. "I don't like comedies."

"It's funny," she assured him. "At least, that's what I was told. You need a night out. You spend too much time working around here. You should hire a manager. You know, I just met a man who would do nicely. He's college educated and . . ."

"I run the ranch," he said coldly, looking up at her.

She hesitated. "Well, I was just mentioning it. About the movie," she added, and quickly changed the subject. He was too quick for her. She'd have to be more careful.

Mallory was remembering the conversation while he was staring pointedly at Morie. She flushed under the scrutiny. He could see her heart beating wildly against her shirt. Her breasts were pointed suddenly, too, and he felt his own body reacting to her arousal. He wanted to back her into the wall and kiss her forever.

He pulled himself up short. He had to get her out of here before he did something stupid. "All right," he said. "You can go back to work."

"Thanks." She didn't look at him again. She could barely walk for the trembly feeling that went over her. He'd looked at her with pure hunger. She knew he wanted her, but he didn't trust her. He was remembering her involuntary outburst in the woods. If only she'd kept her mouth shut! He'd never trust her again and she had only herself to blame. But she could win his trust. She knew she could. She just had to try.

He told Gelly, without meaning to, about Morie's phone call to the Texas judge.

"Well, that's not surprising," she commented on the way to the movie.

"Why not?" he shot at her.

"They were all hugged up together when I went out to tell her to get back to work and stop disturbing your guests," she replied, lying through her teeth. She smiled secretively when she saw his expression. "He was very rude to me. He didn't like it that I interrupted them."

"She said she was giving him a canapé recipe," he scoffed.

She laughed out loud. "Oh, come on!" She glanced at him with lowered eyelids. "And you actually believed her?"

He didn't like feeling foolish. "I suppose so. At first."

"I'm sure there's something going on there," she replied easily. "They obviously knew each other all along. And he's a judge." She glanced at him again. "What if she's trying to set you up for a lawsuit and he's helping her? Some judges are dishonest, you know."

That was what he'd thought himself. He didn't want to agree with her.

"She looks to me the sort who'd look for an easy way," she added. "She's so poor, she'd probably do anything to get out of debt, to have nice clothes that were currently in fashion, to be seen at the best places, to travel first-class around the world." She was daydreaming, not about her rival's wishes, but her own. Her face set in hard lines. "She's probably sick of having to do things she hates just to get ahead in life, to have the things she deserves and can't get any other way."

He gave her an astonished look.

She noted it, and cleared her throat. "I mean, that sort of woman obviously is hoping to make some rich man fall for her, and she'll do whatever it takes. You're rich. Of course she wants you. It's obvious."

"It is?"

"She stares at you all the time," she muttered. "Like a kid looking at the counter in an ice-cream shop."

"She does?" His heart jumped. He had to force himself not to react. "I hadn't noticed," he added in a droll tone.

"It's disgusting the way she falls all over herself to please you. Let me tell you, she's not like that around me," she said grimly. "She's all claws and teeth. She hates me. The way she talks to me . . . you should say something to her about it," she added firmly. "It's not right, to have a hired person speak that way to someone of my class."

Of her class. Her father was a retired textile worker, he'd found that out quite accidentally in conversation with a neighbor. Her late mother had been a bank clerk, an honorable profession but not something that gave her carte blanche to high society. Gelly had aspirations. She wanted money. He felt hunted, all of a sudden. She'd been sweet and clinging and flattering at first. Now she was becoming aggressive and demanding, pushing him toward her friends who wanted cheap land and jobs and other things. It was vaguely annoying.

"You're getting a little pushy lately yourself, Gelly," he remarked curtly.

She caught her breath. "Am I? How so?"

"You sure do know plenty of people I can help," he noted coolly.

She bit her lip. "Oh, that. I was asked about jobs here, that's all. I don't even know the man who wanted the managerial position—he's a friend of a friend. And the man who wants the land is a good friend of my father's. My father worked in a textile corporation, you know. He was quite well-known in certain circles."

He was a cloth cutter, but Mallory wasn't saying it. He'd keep his own counsel. There was something about Gelly that started to ring alarm bells in his brain. He just smiled and asked her where she'd like to eat after the movie let out.

But later he spoke to Tank.

"What do you really think of Gelly?" he asked when they were sipping coffee alone at the kitchen table. They rarely had it late at night, but they were helping with calving and it was a long and tedious job that never seemed to end when it was bedtime.

Tank's dark eyes narrowed. "I don't think about her, if I can help it. Why?"

"She's got a friend who wants us to sell him some scrubland we own, that tract on the northern boundary that we can't run cattle on. She says it's just worthless land. He's down on his luck and wants us to sell it to him cheap."

Tank pursed his lips. "Wasn't that the same land that the oil company had its eye on for fracking and we refused to lease it to them?"

Mallory raised his head. His eyes narrowed. "The very same."

"I wonder if her friend has any ties to the oil and gas industry."

"I wonder," Mallory repeated, and he didn't smile.

"You were asking someone about phone records," Tank added. "May I ask why?"

He shifted restlessly and sipped coffee. "Morie called that superior-court-judge friend of Cane's in Texas late at night."

Tank's eyes lifted. "Danny Brannt?"

Mallory looked murderous. "Brannt?"

"Yes. His brother is Kingston Brannt. He has an empire down in Texas. Runs Santa Gertrudis cattle that make ours look like mongrels by comparison."

"Morie's last name is Brannt," Mallory replied thoughtfully.

"Yes, but there's no relation. I asked Danny. He said it's one of the most common names in his part of Texas." He added with a smile, "Like Smith in other places. Coincidence. Nothing more."

"Really?"

"Look at Morie, for God's sake," Tank replied. "She's sweet, but she's poor as Job's turkey, can't you see? She didn't even have a decent cell phone until we got one for her."

Mallory felt a chill. "She's courting a judge," he said. "I think she may be looking for a way to sue us."

"You tar and feather her every chance you get, don't you?" Tank replied. "I wonder why."

"Gelly thinks she's up to something."

"Yes? Well, I think Gelly's up to something, and to your detriment." He finished his coffee. "Better watch your step."

"Maybe so," he conceded after a minute. He finished his own coffee. "Guess we'd better grab a little sleep while we can," he added.

Tank nodded his agreement. "Good advice."

CHAPTER EIGHT

The next day, Morie found an excuse to talk to Tank after they moved cattle from one pasture to another.

"I need to tell you something. I don't quite know how," she said when they were resting for a minute with thermoses full of coffee while the cattle grazed in their new fenced area.

He pushed his hat back and wiped his sweaty brow with his forearm. "Go ahead."

She glanced around to make sure nobody was near enough to hear. "Joe

Bascomb was at the line cabin," she said.

"What? Good Lord, girl . . . !"

"He didn't hurt me. He didn't even really threaten me," she said. "He was hungry, so I gave him a biscuit and some water. He's in awful shape."

He winced. "He was my friend. I don't believe he could deliberately kill anybody."

"Neither do I. He said that his attorney gave him up when he escaped." She hesitated. "He said there was a relative of the dead man on the jury that convicted him. That should be grounds for a retrial, shouldn't it?"

He glanced at her curiously. "That's why you called the judge in Texas, isn't it?"

She laughed ruefully. "Yes," she admitted.

"What did he say?"

"That it should be grounds for a retrial. But Joe needs to turn himself in, and he needs a new attorney."

"I'd pay for one myself if I could find anybody locally who'd agree to defend him. The dead man's family is much loved here," he added. "Nobody thinks the victim was a valuable member of society, but his family is powerful. Not many local attorneys want the stigma of defending his killer."

"The judge might know somebody who'd do it pro bono," she added.

"What did you do to talk him into that?" he exclaimed.

"I appealed to his sense of justice. He's a very nice man. He came into the kitchen to compliment the cook on the food. Whoever thinks to do that at a party?" she added, having been to dozens where the food was taken for granted.

"He must be a nice man," he agreed with a smile. "I'll see what I can do." He sobered. "But don't you talk to Joe again, regardless of the circumstances. You get on your horse and leave. It's dangerous, abetting an escaped criminal. I think he's innocent, but the court judged him guilty."

"And you'd ride away and refuse help, would you?" she asked placidly.

"Well, no, I wouldn't. But I'm in a different situation than you are." His eyes narrowed. "You work for us. So you do as we say. Got that?"

"Yes, sir," she said with a sigh.

"I'm not trying to be mean. I just want to keep you out of trouble, if I can. You'd better stay clear of Gelly, too," he added. "She's really got it in for you."

"I'm not afraid of her."

"You should be," he replied. "Because Mallory believes the things she tells him. I don't know why. He doesn't even particularly like her. She just flatters his ego. He's never had much luck with women wanting him for himself, and he's easily swayed because of it. He thinks he's ugly."

"Ugly? Mallory?" she exclaimed. "Good heavens, he's not ugly!"

He pursed his lips. "He's not?"

She flushed and cleared her throat. "Well, I'd better get back to work. But I wanted you to know about Joe. I hope somebody can help him."

"Me, too."

She got on her horse and rode off, leaving Tank more puzzled than ever about her.

* * *

Mallory was preoccupied. Gelly gave him a long, searching look while they ate salads at the local restaurant.

"You're worried about something, aren't you?" she asked, smiling.

He shrugged. "My brothers are falling over themselves to help our newest hire," he muttered.

"That woman," Gelly scoffed. She put down her fork. "Mal, she's a con artist if I ever saw one! Why don't you fire her?"

He finished his salad. "I'd be lynched," he mused. "Everybody's crazy about her. Even old Mavie, who hates most people." It made him feel an odd sense of pride that the people who worked for him valued Morie. He didn't know why.

Gelly's blue eyes glittered. "She's going to cause big trouble if you let her stay. You already told me what happened with your brothers when she started playing that piano. How did she learn, do you think? Maybe she played piano in a bar," she suggested with just the right note of suspicion. "What do you really know about her? You should check her out. You really should. I'll bet she has a really terrible background."

"I wonder," he said. It was their policy to check out new hires, and he had. But the detective had run into a stone wall about her family background. She seemed to be without any family in Wyoming. But his investigation had noted that she'd worked for two other ranches and had glowing recommendations from the owners. He couldn't have known that Morie had provided those references deliberately and made sure the people involved were coached in what information to give out. She'd hoped the detective would do only a surface scan and not use her social-security number to derive damaging information. But, then, the privacy laws would prevent most of that incursion without proof of criminal intent. And she'd never broken the law. She didn't even have a parking or speeding ticket to her name.

"I think she's trying to trick you into having a relationship with her," Gelly suggested. "I've seen the way she looks at you. She wants you." She leaned forward earnestly. "She would love to be pregnant. You'd have to support her and the child or she'd go to the authorities. Maybe even the television stations! What a pathetic picture she could paint, about being victimized by her boss!"

He took that with a grain of salt. But what Gelly said made sense, especially in light of his last, urgent moment with her, the hired help. He felt shamed by his lack of control, and he was still suspicious about Morie's whispered desire for a child.

Gelly saw his indecision. She would have to act. The woman was getting to Mal, and she was going to lose him if she didn't get her off the place. She had plans, big plans, for Mal and this ranch. All she needed was a little more time. She had a friend who wanted to make a huge development on land Mal owned. She was being cut in for a small fortune. All she had to do was ease Mal into a nice relationship and then convince him to give up those few worthless acres to her for a pittance. After all, it was scrubland; he didn't even run cattle on it. Her friend had connections to the gas industry and he wanted the land for fracking, to drill through shale deposits to force oil to the surface. He'd checked out geological surveys, and that land was rich in oil and gas deposits, worth a fortune, in fact!

It was a controversial technique that had, on occasion, polluted local water tables to the extent that water could be set on fire with a match, because of the gas that infiltrated the water. But that wasn't Gelly's concern; she only wanted the kickback she was promised. It would be formidable. Then she could buy anything she wanted, instead of wearing things from a consignment shop. Fortunately for her, the brothers knew nothing about fashion and didn't realize that she was only pretending the sophistication they saw. She had other plans, even bigger ones, once she cajoled Mal into marrying her. That would take more time. But Morie was a threat and she had to be removed.

It would be easy enough. Mal already distrusted the new hire, and Morie was as dim as a low-battery flashlight. All Gelly had to do was play up to one of the young cowboys who liked her and watched her whenever she was around. A few sweet words, a few kisses, and he'd do whatever she asked. She'd already gained his confidence, pretended affection and concern for him, brought him presents. Little presents, cheap ones, like a ring with his initials on it. But they did the trick. She could use him to help her.

Mal hated a thief more than anything. She smiled. It would be easy.

Morie was helping Darby doctor a sick bull. The bull didn't want help and made his resistance obvious by trying to kick both of them.

"Come on, now, old fellow," Darby said gently as he turned the bull around. "That sore place is infected, and it's not going to get better without help. The vet said to put this on twice a day and we're doing it, whether you like it or not!"

"He really doesn't like that salve." Morie chuckled. "Oof!" she exclaimed when he shifted and knocked her down into the hay.

"You okay?" Darby asked, worried.

"Sure, just winded."

"Hey, Bates, come over here and help us!" he called to a young cowboy who'd just entered the barn.

"Sure thing," he called. "Just let me put away this horse. Ms. Bruner went riding and I showed her some of the good paths." He flushed, remembering how sweet that ride had been. "She's a real nice lady."

Darby and Morie gaped at him. He didn't notice. He was still floating. Gelly had kissed him and whispered that she would do anything he liked if he would just do one little thing for her. All he had to do was place a priceless jeweled egg she'd taken from the Kirks' living room in Morie's rucksack. Such a small favor. She wasn't going to get the girl in trouble; it had been Cane's idea. It was a practical joke, nothing more . . . would he help? Of course he would!

He chatted to Morie as he helped them with the reluctant bull. Boy, was Miss Morie in for a surprise, he thought merrily. She was a good sport. He didn't know why Cane wanted to play a trick on her, but then, he didn't understand rich people and their senses of humor in the first place.

"Thanks, Bates," Darby told him when they were finished. "You're a good man."

"No problem," he replied. "I love ranch work, even the dirty bits."

"Me, too," Morie agreed, laughing. "It's nice to be out in the open and not to work a nine-to-five job shut up in an office somewhere."

"That's why I like it here so much." Bates nodded. "Good land, fine cattle, nice people."

"Lots of nice people," Morie agreed, and smiled at Darby.

He returned her smile. "Okay, back to work. We'd better leave before Old Stomper here finds a way to corner us and kick us. Had that happen before. He sure hates being touched."

"Old Stomper?" Morie questioned

when Bates had gone back to the horses.

"He likes to step on cowboys," he explained. "Broke a man's foot during roundup." He shook his head. "He's one bad customer. But he's the best breeding bull we've got, so he gets pampered."

"That's Kirk's Ransom 428, isn't he?" she wondered aloud.

His eyes almost popped. "Yes, how did you know?"

"I, uh, look at sales papers." She faltered. "I recognized him from his conformation."

Darby was speechless.

"I've been around cattlemen all my life," she said after a minute. "Certainly long enough to know a prize bull when I see one. I just didn't recognize him while I was trying to keep from being shoved to death," she added ruefully.

He gave a short laugh and gave up his suspicions. "Sure. I can understand that."

"I guess I'd better get back out to the line cabin . . ."

"Miss Brannt!"

She and Darby turned at the cold and belligerent address.

"Yes, sir, boss?" she asked.

His eyes were as cold as his face was hard. "Come to the bunkhouse, please." He turned and walked out.

"The bunkhouse?" she wondered aloud. She went out with Darby and noticed that Bates was smothering a grin.

Darby went with her. He knew the boss's moods. That look was dangerous. He'd seen it before, when the cook, Vanessa, had been fired. He had a bad feeling and he looked at Morie with concern.

They walked into the bunkhouse. Mallory was there, with Ms. Bruner and Cane and Tank. None of them were smiling.

"Open your rucksack, please," Mallory asked curtly.

She lifted both eyebrows. "Sure. But why?" she asked as she retrieved it from her room and handed it to the boss.

"Open it, please," he repeated.

She shrugged, put it down on the table near the door and opened it. She pulled out clothing, books and . . .

Her expression was genuinely shocked. That was a replica of one of the famous Romanov Easter eggs that had originally been made for the czar of Russia and his wife. It was made of pure gold, which was going for over a thousand dollars a gram at current market prices, and studded with diamonds and sapphires, rubies and emeralds. It was worth a king's ransom. She held it in her hand and gaped at it. She'd last seen it in the Kirks' living room in a locked case. How . . . ?

She turned and looked at them. Ms. Bruner wasn't smiling, but there was a look on her face that made Morie want to put her out a window.

"This egg was left to us by our grandmother, who was given it as a Christmas gift from her husband decades ago," Mallory said with ice dripping from every syllable. "It's utterly priceless."

"At current gold prices, the gold alone would buy a Jaguar," she murmured, shocked.

"Interesting, that a poor working cowgirl would know that," Mallory replied.

She handed the egg to Mallory. Her eyes were full of abused pride. "You think that I would steal from you?" she asked quietly, and searched his face.

"The evidence pretty much speaks for itself," Mallory told her.

She looked from his angry face to Cane's shocked one and Tank's bland one. Darby lifted his chin.

"She's no thief," Darby said shortly. "I may not be the world's best judge of character, but I'd bet my retirement on this girl's honesty. Saw her run down a cowboy who dropped a five-dollar bill out of his wallet and didn't notice. Not the act of a thief," he added.

"This was missing out of the case." Mallory indicated the egg.

"How did she get the key?" Tank asked aloud.

"Mine is missing," Mallory said coldly. His eyes narrowed on Morie.

She just stared at him, with her heart breaking in her chest. She was damned without a trial. Everybody was looking at her with varying degrees of suspicion. She knew she'd been set up and she knew who did it—that Bruner woman, with some help, she would have bet, from that grinning cowboy in the barn who'd gone riding with her. Bates.

But it would do no good to condemn him on a stray thought. Nothing she said was going to convince Mallory that she'd been set up. She could see that in his face. It twisted her heart. If he'd cared for her at all, he'd never have believed her capable of this.

She stared at him with resignation. "I suppose you want to call the sheriff now," she said, and thought how she was going to explain this to her parents. Her father would be outraged. He'd come after Mallory with his team of family attorneys and it would be a major assault on the man's reputation and wealth. Her father was vindictive. Especially where his children were concerned. Mallory Kirk had no idea what a hornet's nest he was stirring up, nor did that Bruner woman, whose entire past would be laid out to public view when her dad got through.

"No," Mallory said, averting his eyes. "I won't do that. But you're resigning as of right now. I want you off my land in one hour. No more. And Darby will watch you pack, to make sure nothing else goes mysteriously missing."

Morie lifted her chin. Spanish royalty from three generations ago showed itself in her comportment and arrogance. "I have never stolen anything in my life," she said with quiet pride. "And you will regret this. I promise you."

"Threats!" Gelly scoffed. "The last resort of a thief caught red-handed!"

"You remember it," Morie told her evenly. "You're wearing last year's clothes, probably bought from a consignment shop, and trying to insinuate yourself into the boss's life," she said flatly, shocking everybody, especially Gelly. "You're a fraud, too, lady. I don't know what your game is, but sooner or later, you'll betray yourself."

Gelly moved closer to Mallory. There was something oddly dangerous in the other woman's delicate features. Something Gelly recognized, because she'd seen it before.

"How would you know anything about fashion?" Mallory asked coldly, indicating Morie's stained and torn jeans and old sweatshirt and disheveled condition.

"You might be surprised at what I know, and where I learned it," she told him. Her black eyes were snapping like fireworks under her long, black eyelashes. "One day you'll know the truth about me, too. And you'll regret to your dying day that you ever accused me of a crime."

"Criminals always say such things," Gelly chided.

Morie smiled coldly. "You'd know."

"How dare you!" Gelly stepped forward with her hand raised.

"Lawsuits will ensue if you hit me," Morie told her. "I promise."

Mallory caught the woman's arm and pulled her back. "Let's get this over without complications," he told her. He was feeling really sick at what he'd charged Morie with. He hadn't even let her speak.

"If you have a defense, let's hear it," he added, his eyes on hers.

Morie just laughed. "Sure. I've been set up and she—" she indicated Gelly "—knows it. But nobody is going to believe me. I'm just the new hire."

She put her things into the rucksack and gathered up her small television and iPod and coat. "This is all I brought with me. May I ask someone to drive me to the bus station in town, or would you like me to walk there?" she added icily.

Mallory felt even worse when he saw how little she had. Maybe she'd been desperate for money. But if she had, why not come to him and ask for help? His face hardened. He'd made that impossible, with his own antagonism.

"I'll drive you, honey," Cane said gently. "Let's go."

"I can drive her," Tank protested.

Neither of them believed her guilty, and it was obvious.

"Thanks," Morie told them sincerely. "I'll remember you both kindly, years from now."

Mallory was fuming. He hated being

put in this position. And he really hated having his own brothers make him look like the villain.

"Darby, could you drive me to town, please?" she asked the older man. "If the boss doesn't mind."

"Drive her," Mallory said curtly. He glared at his brothers. "In case you didn't notice, she had Grandmother's jeweled egg in her rucksack!"

Both brothers looked at Gelly with veiled hostility.

She stepped closer to Mallory. "Why are you looking at me? I didn't steal anything!"

"Neither did I," Morie told her as Darby gathered up the heavy things and she shouldered her pack. She smiled at Gelly. It wasn't a nice smile. "When I get home, my father will want to know all about you," she added softly. "I'm sure he'll find interesting things."

Gelly panicked for just a minute. But she noted the other woman's pitiful clothing and lost her worry. "Oh, I'm sure." She laughed. "Does he even own a computer?"

You might be surprised, Morie thought, but she didn't speak. She looked up at Mallory as she passed him, with sadness and pain.

"You might have given me the benefit of the doubt," she said quietly.

"I did," he muttered.

She sighed. "You think I stole from you," she said in a soft, wounded tone.

"You did," he replied, digging in.

She shook her head. "One day, you'll find out the truth and you'll be sorry. But it will be too late," she added.

He felt cold chills down his spine. He wasn't in the wrong. Gelly had assured him that one of the hands knew something that he was afraid to tell. She'd learned about it accidentally while they were riding. The poor boy was almost in tears as he related how he'd seen Morie handling that beautiful egg he'd once seen in the display case inside the big ranch house. Of course, unbeknownst to him, Gelly had coaxed Bates into going to Mallory with his story and coached him on how to behave.

Mallory felt sick to his stomach. Morie was going to leave. He'd never see her again. It shouldn't bother him. He knew she was after him for his money; no woman had ever wanted him for any other reason. He knew he wasn't handsome. She was a gold digger. Why did it hurt so damned much to see that pain in her face, to hear it in her voice?

"If you're leaving, go," he said curtly. "Before I change my mind and have you prosecuted!"

"Oh, that would be very interesting," Morie replied with a twinge of her old audacity. "Very interesting, indeed. In fact, I'm quite tempted to dare you to do it," she added with a thoughtful look at Gelly, who was flushed and worried.

"No!" Gelly said, feeling suddenly unsure of herself at the other woman's confident smile. She was friends with the judge who knew Cane. She might dig up something that Gelly didn't want known. "No, it's too much. She's poor. Just let her go. One day, she'll get what's coming to her."

"More than likely, you will," Morie

countered. She looked at the brothers. "I enjoyed my time here."

"I don't think you did it," Cane said flatly.

"Neither do I," Tank affirmed.

They both glared at Mallory.

"Well, she's got you blindsided," Mallory shot back. "What, you didn't notice the egg in her rucksack, huh? It got there by magic, I guess."

They started to argue, but she got between them. "I've caused enough trouble," she told them. "I guess I'll have to go back and take the consequences." She meant go back and let her father arrange that marriage to his best friend's son, who was a millionaire twice over and had a flourishing feedlot operation in North Texas. It would make for a great partnership.

"In trouble at home, are you?" Mallory asked curtly.

"Usually," she replied. "Thanks for the job," she added, and not with a great deal of sarcasm. "I learned a lot here." She turned to Darby. "Mostly from you," she said with a smile. "I'll miss you."

"I'll miss you, too," Darby said with a cold look at Mallory as he left.

She turned to continue out the door. She stopped, turned back to Mallory and glared up at him. "I won't miss you," she replied harshly. "I was totally wrong. I thought you were the last person on earth who would have convicted me on circumstantial evidence. But then, I can't expect a stranger to care about me. I had dreams . . ." Her eyes fell. "Foolish dreams. Anyway, take care, guys," she told the other two brothers and managed a smile for them. "See you someday, maybe."

They grimaced and turned back to glare at Mallory. But Morie was already in the ranch pickup with Darby at the wheel. Headed home to Texas.

"You mark my words, that woman had something to do with it," Cane said angrily. "She set Morie up."

"I agree," Tank replied. "We should have stopped her from leaving. We should have made Mal listen."

"He won't. He was infatuated with Morie. He didn't like it. He wanted to believe she was a thief, so he had an excuse to fire her." He turned to his brother. "She almost dared him to prosecute her. Would a thief be willing to go to trial?"

"Not likely. I remember Joe Bascomb saying that he was anxious for his case to go to trial so he'd be cleared in the eyes of the community. Of course, we see how that played out!" His eyes narrowed as he looked toward the barn. "Interesting, how Bates just happened to notice Morie playing with that egg. She lives in a separate room, and the door's always closed, Darby said. So how did he see her?"

"And what the hell was he doing, riding around with Mal's girlfriend?" Cane added. "Something fishy there. Real fishy. It was Gelly who just happened to find the missing drill in our former employee's suitcase. And now, surprise, surprise, she just happened to hear a cowboy who noticed a thief playing with a rare objet d'art. How convenient."

Tank pursed his lips. "I really think we need to do some investigating of our own. I still have contacts in government, some of them covert operatives. It wouldn't take much work to look into Ms. Bruner's background, now would it?"

"Mal will never believe anything bad about her."

"Think so? Let's find out."

"I'm game. Go for it."

Morie, unaware of the brothers' plotting, was on the bus to Jackson to get a commercial flight home. She hadn't let Darby see her buy the bus ticket to Jackson, because she was supposed to be going back to Texas. And in fact, she was, on her father's corporate jet. It would be waiting for her at the Jackson airport.

She didn't want to tell her parents what had happened for a number of reasons. First, it would be humiliating to have them know that their daughter had been accused of stealing. Second, her father would plow into the Kirks like an earthmover. He'd never stop until he'd utilized every legal resource at his command, and Gelly Bruner would be nailed to the wall, along with whoever had helped her set Morie up.

It had to be Bates, Morie decided. The stupid man was crazy about Gelly. God knew what she'd told him to make him help, but Morie couldn't get that odd smile out of her mind. How strange, for Bates to look at her with that smile and then, shortly afterward, for her to be fired for theft. He'd been with Gelly all morning. Gelly had also set up a former hand who was fired for stealing. It was all so useless.

Of course, nobody knew who Morie really was, or her real background. If they had, Gelly would have had her own head on the block. Morie was rich beyond the dreams of avarice. Gelly, however, would love to be rich. She just wanted to marry Mallory, so that she'd have whatever she wanted. Morie had been in the way. Gelly had been jealous of her from the start, and she had to know that Mallory was feeling something more than professional regard for his newest hire.

Those hungry kisses had knocked Morie off guard. She'd never expected that things would end like this. She choked back tears of anger and loss. Maybe it was just as well, she told herself. Mallory believed in her guilt. If he'd cared about her, nothing would have convinced him that she'd take something from him. That was absolute proof that anything he felt was just physical. He didn't care about Morie. He couldn't have cared, and treated her so coldly.

She dabbed at her eyes with her battered handkerchief. Her father was going to be livid when he found out where she'd been. But Shelby would stand up for her. It would be all right. She'd just have to get through the next few days and it would start getting better. She'd go on with her life, and Mallory would fade into the past, day by day, hour by hour. Maybe in a year she wouldn't even be able to remember what he looked like. Time was kind.

Her father and mother were waiting at the ranch's airstrip. They were standing close together, as they always were, smiling at each other until Morie came down the steps of the small jet.

"Morie!" Shelby ran to her and embraced her, hugging her close. "Oh, it's so good to have you home again!"

"Been rolling in wheat straw?" her father asked, his black eyes that were so much like her own narrowed in suspicion.

She grinned and hugged him tight. "Yes, I have. Don't fuss, Daddy."

He hugged her, laughing. "Okay. Good to have you home, brat." He held her at arm's length. "Now. Where the hell have you been for the past few weeks?"

She sighed. "Working on a ranch as a cowgirl," she confessed.

"Good God Almighty!" he raged. "Hell, I wouldn't even let you lift a hay bale here and you went to work on a . . . !"

"Please don't fuss," she interrupted. "I learned so much about ranching. I learned about calving and feed and fences, all the things you'd never teach me. I learned ranching from the ground up. And I had a good time doing it."

"Where did you work?" he persisted.

"In Wyoming, for people who had no idea who I was," she said. "And that's all I'm going to say about it. Ever."

"Was it a big ranch?" he asked.

She shrugged. "A family one."

"I see."

"Some brothers. They were nice. I even had my own room in the bunkhouse and all the cowboys looked out for me. It was just like here, only smaller," she added, to cover herself. "Much smaller."

"Did you tell them who you were when you left?" Shelby wondered.

"No. I just said I had to come home." She dropped her eyes.

Shelby, who knew her very well, was certain that there was much more to this story that Morie didn't want to tell her parents.

"Well, we can talk about it later." Shelby said gently. She smiled at King. "Right now, let's get her home and cleaned up. Honestly, Morie, you do look ragged!"

Morie laughed. "It was fun, while it lasted."

"It's nice to have you home." Shelby sighed, hugging her again. "I'm surrounded by men when you aren't here. Nobody wants to discuss recipes or Paris sales and shopping."

King made a face. "I'll talk about the production sale late this month," he volunteered.

Shelby glowered at him. "I'm already tired of hearing about it. Who do you think is having to make all the arrangements, my darling? Not you! I'll bet you have no clue about caterers and musical entertainment and tables and chairs and awnings. . . ."

"Gosh, is that the time?" King glanced at his big watch. "I have cattle to brand!"

Shelby made a face at him. "Then you can drop us off at the house on your way," she told him with a chuckle.

He smiled back. He shouldered the box and the rucksack that Morie had brought with her and headed for the big ranch SUV.

Later, Shelby cornered her daughter in the bedroom and closed the door.

"You can fool your dad," she said,

"but you can't ever fool me. Now come clean," she told Morie and sat down beside her on the spotless comforter with its exquisite pastel floral design. "What really happened?"

Morie laid her head on Shelby's shoulder. "I fell in love."

"Really!"

"He was a beast. He had a girlfriend who was pretending to be something she's not. She had someone plant a jeweled egg in my rucksack and went to the boss and told him I stole it from him. So he fired me. I came home. End of story."

"He accused you of theft?" she exclaimed.

"Yes. He said he wouldn't call the sheriff, but he fired me."

Shelby's dark eyes flashed. "We'll sue him for defamation of character!"

"No, you won't," Morie said calmly. "It would be useless. That woman set me up. I can't prove it, but I know she did it. He believed her," she added with a pointed look at her mother. "No man who loved a woman would ever convict her on circumstantial evidence, no matter how damning it was."

Shelby drew in a long breath. In a minute, she nodded. "If that's the way you want it."

"Please don't tell Daddy."

Shelby grimaced. "I have to tell him something."

"Then embroider it a little, can't you?" She knew that her parents never had secrets from each other. She envied them their closeness. She felt now that she'd never have anyone to share secrets with.

"I'll soft-pedal it," Shelby promised. "But I don't like it. You're no thief."

"We know it. We don't have to prove it to anyone."

"That's true enough. But I'd like to jerk a knot in your boss, and his girlfriend," Shelby added. She wasn't a fiery woman, but she did have a temper.

Morie hugged her. "Thanks."

"You're my daughter. I love you." She kissed her cheek. She frowned. "What in the world happened to your face?"

"Just a scratch. I was moving a tree

branch and it shifted. It's only a surface one. It will heal nicely, you'll see. Now how about a nice piece of broiled fish with herbs and butter? Please?"

Shelby laughed. "All right. Just for you. A homecoming present. I'm glad you're back."

"Yes." Morie sighed as she looked around at familiar things. "So am I."

CHAPTER NINE

Morie threw herself into helping Shelby with details for the big production sale. In between, she had to cope with her father's matchmaking. Daryl Coleman was tall and dark and quite good-looking. His family had huge feedlots in Northern Texas and Daryl himself was CEO of an oil company that was based in Oklahoma. He was savvy about technical innovations and a whiz with computers. He had everything a woman could have wanted. He just wasn't Mallory Kirk.

But he liked Morie and he was always around. After Mallory's suspicion and alternating hot-and-cold treatment, Daryl was a breath of fresh air. He had exquisite manners and he loved to dance. So did Morie. It was one of the things she loved most in life.

Daryl flew her to Dallas in the corporate jet that his family had shares in, and took her to an authentic Latin dance club.

"So you want to learn to tango," he told her with a grin. "This is the place to learn."

"I'm not keen on it," she mumbled, looking around. "It looks a whole lot easier in movies."

"None of the movies it's in are authentic," he assured her. He took her right hand in his left one and rested his free hand on her waist. "Tango is a battle between a man and a woman. It's quick and slow, insistent and sensuous. Most of it is footwork. Just follow my lead. You're an excellent dancer. This should be easy for you."

"Easy!" she scoffed after she'd stumbled into him three times and almost upset a waiter with a tray of drinks headed for the restaurant at the other end of the club. No alcohol was allowed near the dance floor itself.

He chuckled. "You're rusty, kid," he teased. "You've been spending too much time around cattle and not enough around attractive, dashing men like me."

She looked up at his good looks and twinkling dark eyes and burst out laughing. "And so modest!"

"I'm modest. After all, I have so much to be modest about," he assured her.

She leaned against him with a breathless laugh. "Daryl, you're a wonder."

He hugged her close. "Sure I am. You really need to marry me," he added with a smile. "Your father says so every time he sees me."

She grimaced. "I like you a lot, but my dad is looking at mergers, not relationships. It's a flat economy and he's diversifying his investments. Like your folks," she added drily.

He shrugged. "I haven't met anybody I really want to marry," he said honestly. "You're pretty and sweet, and you won't be marrying me for my money," he added in a cold tone.

She stopped dancing and looked up. "Somebody did want to marry you for it," she guessed.

He nodded. "She was sweet and pretty, too. I went nuts over her. Then, just before I was getting ready to propose, I saw her at a party sneaking into a bedroom with the host. They came back out a few minutes later, disheveled and laughing, and when I asked, she said sure she slept with him. He'd given her a diamond dinner ring and she wanted to pay him back for it." His face hardened. "She said everybody did it, why was I so uptight? It was just sex."

Morie searched his black eyes quietly. "That's the attitude most people have today. Everything is okay now. Multiple lovers are the rule. Funny, isn't it, that fifty years ago men and women alike were held to a higher standard of morality and families stayed together. Isn't the divorce rate something like fifty percent?"

"Probably higher." He sighed. "I'm so

old-fashioned that I don't fit in anywhere."

"So am I, sweet man," she replied,
and pressed close to him, closing her
eyes. "Maybe I should marry you, Daryl. We're alike in a lot of ways. I really
do like you."

He hugged her close. "I like you, too,
honey. I guess there are worse reasons
to base a marriage on."

She kept her eyes closed as they
danced and tried not to think about
how it had felt when Mallory held her
close and kissed her in that incredibly
sexy way and made her head spin.
Maybe it would be safer to marry a man
she only liked. Passionate love surely
made life more complicated.

He kissed her hair. "What kind of ring
would you like?" he asked matter-of-
factly.

She drew in a long breath. "I don't
know. Maybe a ruby. I like rubies."

"Coincidentally, my family has investments in a jewelry chain," he teased.
"So you can have whatever stone you
fancy, and we'll have a designer make
it into your dream wedding set."

Her dream wedding set would have included Mallory as the groom, but she couldn't say that. She was falling into her father's net headfirst, letting him rule her life. She'd tried rebellion, however, and it had ended badly. Very badly. It might be time to listen to her father's advice and do something sensible. After all, Daryl was highly eligible and quite good-looking, and they'd known each other for a long time. It wouldn't be a passionate relationship. But it would be a lasting one, she was certain.

Now all she had to do was stop thinking about Mallory Kirk. That wasn't going to be easy.

Mallory was having problems of his own. His brothers refused to be in the same room with Gelly, and when she came to the ranch, they made their disapproval known by walking away the minute her small used car pulled up at the front porch.

"Do you have to make it so obvious that you don't like her?" Mallory raged to Cane.

Cane gave him a cold look. "She framed Morie."

"Damn it, she did not! Gelly just happened to be riding with Bates when he mentioned what he'd seen."

"Like she just happened to know about the stolen drill in our former employee's suitcase," Cane retorted. "Anybody who makes Gelly mad gets fired."

Mallory averted his dark eyes. "Coincidence."

Cane stuck his hand in his pocket and went to the picture window to look out over the acres of green pasture just starting to stick up through the latest snow. "And I won't agree to let her friend buy that so-called scrubland, in case you were going to ask."

"Neither will I," Tank added curtly as he joined them.

Mallory didn't reply. He'd had Gelly harping on it for days. He was almost ready to sell it just to get her off his back. When she wasn't being obnoxious, she was sweeter than she'd ever been. She caressed him and kissed him and told him how handsome he was, and how happy she was that he'd been saved from that money-grubbing girl he'd had to fire.

For a man whose lack of conventional good looks was imposing, it was an ego trip of the finest kind. It blinded him to her other faults. He wouldn't concede that he was vulnerable because he was guilt-ridden over firing Morie on flimsy circumstantial evidence.

"Did that key to the display case ever show up?" Cane asked suddenly and with narrowed eyes.

Mallory joined him at the picture window, his hands jammed deep into his jean pockets. "Yeah," he replied. "Found it in my coat pocket. I guess I forgot and put it there instead of back in the drawer where we keep it."

"Odd," Tank commented.

And Gelly knew about the key and where it was kept, because she'd admired that egg once and Mallory had pulled out the key to open the case and let her hold it. He didn't mention that.

They moved to the display case and studied the egg.

"You know," Mallory said suddenly, frowning, "it looks funny."

"I was just noticing that," Cane replied curtly. "Open it."

Mallory brought the key out of the drawer and opened the glass doors of the ornate, wood-scrolled cabinet. He picked up the egg and frowned. "These settings look slipshod. And here—" he indicated the jewels "—they don't look . . . Good God, it's a fake!"

Cane's jaw tautened. "A cheap fake."

Mallory was seething. "Morie," he said flatly. "She had the real one in her rucksack."

"She handed it back to you," Tank replied angrily. "You put it back in the case. I saw you do it. Morie was gone by then!"

Mallory didn't want to admit that. It suited him to think Morie was a thief. He'd sent her packing, wounded her pride, treated her like a criminal, all on the word of a cowboy he hardly knew and a woman who harried him night and day to employ her friends and sell land to them.

His lean face was harassed. "Yes," he had to concede, his eyes stormy. "She was gone by then."

And all the joy in his life had gone with her. He was left with the emptiness in his heart and the certainty of long years ahead with Gelly to assuage the ache Morie had left behind. She couldn't do it. He liked Gelly, but she didn't stir him, not even with her most passionate kisses, except in the most basic way. Intellectually, she was a no-show. Her conversational skills revolved around popular television shows and movies and the latest fashions.

"It's time to call in private detectives," Cane said flatly. "In fact, Morie advised that some time ago, when I talked to her at the line cabin."

Mallory glared at him. "What were you doing out there?"

His brother smiled coldly. "Looking for Morie after you'd upset her."

"She was a hire. She stuck her nose into everything around here," he muttered.

"Yes, like making canapés for a party and helping cook—and she didn't even ask for extra pay or complain that she didn't get it," Tank reminded him.

Mallory felt guilty. "I meant to compensate her for that. Of course, she was running around after that judge friend of yours," he added icily, turning to Cane.

"Danny Brannt is a gourmet chef," Cane replied. "He and his wife have a housekeeper who was trained in Paris as a cook, and they're always looking for new and exciting finger foods for parties. In fact, they're famous for it. I understand that his housekeeper is helping to cater that big to-do at the Brannt Ranch next month. We were invited, I believe."

"Yes," Mallory murmured absently. "King Brannt has some seed bulls that are the talk of the industry. I have in mind to buy one from him for our breeding program." He didn't add that the mention of that last name stung. Not that Morie had any connection to that famous Brannt; she was just a poor working cowgirl.

"Can we afford one?" Cane asked amusedly. "We're only just showing profit from the past two painful years of investments and stock adjustments."

"We can afford one," Mallory replied

quietly. He glanced at his brother. "You and Tank are responsible for those successes as much as I am," he added. "I know it's been rough. I appreciate what you've done."

"Hell, I appreciate what you've done," Cane said. "You've got the business head. Tank may be the marketing specialist, and I do like showing off our bulls at cattle shows with a little help from our cowboys who travel with me, but you're the one with the genius to know where to put the money so that it will grow. That's no mean feat in a flat economy."

"I had help. Our stockbroker is the genius. I just followed his suggestions." He looked worried. "Who could have taken that egg?" he wondered aloud. "And when did it go missing?"

"I don't know. Sometime between the time that Morie left and you found the key. The question is, who had the key and the opportunity to get into the cabinet?"

"Couldn't have been a break-in," Mallory said, thinking out loud. "Not with our security system in place."

"And I'd bet my stock portfolio on Mavie's honesty," Tank added.

Mallory nodded. "So would I. Her former boss isn't the sort to suffer a thief any more than we are. She was with him for twenty years until he had to give up his ranch and retire, leaving her unemployed. She's been a welcome addition to our staff."

Cane pursed his sensual lips. "Bates, maybe?" He was thinking out loud. "He was the one who claimed to see Morie playing with the egg. Interesting, because Darby says she kept her door closed anytime she was in the bunkhouse, and she kept it locked."

"Suspicious," Mallory said flatly.

"A woman in a bunkhouse full of men would lock her door," Cane shot back. "Especially one like Morie. Darby told me that she lived off campus when she was in college, because she refused to live in a coed dorm even if the whole world thought it was all right."

His eyebrows arched. "She could have been lying."

"Why do you think she lied in the first

place?" Cane demanded. "Because Gelly said she did?"

"Let's not bring Gelly into this," Mallory said defensively. "I'm very fond of her." He pushed his hands deeper into his pockets. "She's having all sorts of financial problems because her father made bad investments." He shrugged. "Maybe I should marry her. . . ."

"I'm leaving the day she comes in the door," Cane said harshly. "And Tank will go with me."

"In a heartbeat," Tank agreed. "We'll take our share of the ranch profits with us," he added in a cold tone. "You and Gelly try staying afloat financially with only a third of the land and cattle!"

"You wouldn't do that," Mallory returned, wounded.

"I'd do it in a heartbeat," Tank assured him with flashing brown eyes.

"So would I," Cane agreed. "I'm not living with Gelly."

"What has she ever done to make you two so hostile?" Mallory exclaimed, exasperated.

Cane looked at Tank. "Blind as a bat."

"And stubborn as a mule," Tank agreed. "Can't tell pyrite from gold."

"Morie stole the egg," Mallory roared. "She took it and hid it in her rucksack and was going to sell it!"

"Sure." Cane took the fake egg in his hand and showed it to Tank. "And she replaced it with this one after we put it back in the cabinet," he added with a droll look at his brother. "Of course, she was on her way home in a bus at the time. I guess it's magic."

Tank nodded. "And funny thing, the key reappeared in Mal's coat pocket."

"How convenient."

"Gelly couldn't have taken the egg," Mallory said doggedly, answering a charge they hadn't made verbally. "She hasn't ever been alone in here!"

"We had a conference call from the state cattlemen's association committee on grazing," Cane reminded him. "All three of us went into the office to take it. Mavie was in the kitchen cooking dinner and Gelly was in here alone. As soon as we came back, she said she had an urgent matter to attend to in town."

Mallory felt sick. "It couldn't be her," he protested, but it was a weak protest.

"If you believe her innocent, let's prove it," Cane said. "I know the best private detective in the business, Dane Lassiter from Houston. Let me have him do some investigating for us. If Gelly has nothing to hide, it will clear her."

"And if not," Tank put in, "it's better to know now, especially if you're bullheaded enough to try and marry her."

"She loves me," Mallory bit off. "She says she can't live without me." He averted his eyes. "She thinks I'm handsome."

"Nobody thinks you're handsome who isn't lying," Cane told him flatly. "Look in a mirror! But looks have nothing to do with character, and you've got plenty of that. Women don't care about looks. They care about actions."

Mallory glared at him.

"He's right." Tank clapped him on the back. "We love you. We won't lie to you. But you might ask yourself why Gelly is. And why she keeps trying to get jobs for her friends and land for some stranger that she barely knows."

Mallory was weakening. He'd been stubborn because he was guilt-ridden about the way he'd treated Morie. His brothers were right. Morie couldn't have taken the egg. She left the ranch just minutes after it was found in her rucksack, and Mallory was certain that he'd held the real egg in his hands in the bunkhouse. He'd put it back in the display case himself, after Morie was gone. So the real one had to have been replaced after Morie's departure . . . replaced with this cheap copy that would only have fooled someone from a distance. None of them had thought to look at it closely. There had been no reason to.

"Let me call Dane," Cane coaxed. "If you're right about Gelly, I'll apologize."

"So will I," Tank agreed.

Mallory drew in a long breath. "Okay," he said after a minute. His expression was grim. "Call him."

The estate was brilliant with color and decoration, especially the huge stone patio where tables were going to be set up the following week for King's gala production show. Ranchers were coming from all over the world to look at his prize cattle, which would be offered for sale at auction.

"Dad really does things on a big scale," Morie mused as she and her mother went over the final plans with a staff of professionals who would complete the finishing touches and employ caterers for the occasion. It was much too large an endeavor for any one person, although Shelby kept a tight rein on the operation and dictated what she wanted done.

"Yes, he does," Shelby said with a smile. "He's very proud of his purebred herd."

"So am I," Morie replied. "Now that I know how a ranch operates from the ground up, I have even more admiration for the care Dad takes of his cattle and his men."

"My daughter, the cowgirl," Shelly chuckled.

"I enjoyed it. Most of it," she replied and lowered her eyes.

Shelby turned back to the woman who was carrying out the party plans. "You were able to get Desperado to play for us, weren't you?"

Tenny Welsh laughed. "Yes, I was," she said, "although the group is semi-retired now. They all have kids and touring isn't conducive to raising a family, they say. But they'll do it for you," she told Shelby. "Heather Everett is best friends with the lead singer. She convinced them."

"God bless her," Shelby said fervently. "She's such a sweetie."

"So is her daughter, Odalie," Tenny replied with a sigh. "Have you ever heard her sing? She has the voice of an angel!"

"Where did you hear her?" Morie asked, curious.

"She goes to our church and is a soloist in the choir," the other woman replied with a smile. "It's such a joy to hear her."

"She's had an offer from the Met, by the way," Shelby told Morie. "She's deliberating whether or not to go."

"It would be a shame to waste a talent like that," the caterer replied dreamily. "Oh, I'd love to have such a voice!"

Morie didn't reply. She was thinking of her brother, Cort, who had such a hopeless passion for the shy blonde, who apparently hated him. Nobody knew why. Well, perhaps Cort did, but he was very tight-lipped about his private life.

"So here's the final menu." Shelby interrupted her thoughts as she handed the printed list to the caterer. "And please make certain that we have a variety of canapés to suit every taste, and plenty of fruit."

"I always do," Tenny reminded her with a smile. This wasn't the first time she'd catered big social parties for the Brannts. "I know your tastes very well, Shelby."

Shelby laughed. "It will be a gala occasion. We have a famous soccer star, four A-list actors and actresses, the CEO of a giant computer/software corporation, two government agents, a few assorted mercenaries and the former vice president."

"Vice president?" Morie asked, surprised.

"He's a friend of your father's," she replied. "Of course, so are the mercenaries," she added amusedly. "He likes black sheep."

"Well, they are interesting people," Tenny added. Her face changed. "Especially that man, Grange, who works for the Pendletons. The stories I've heard about him!"

"Yes, he was a former major in the Green Berets," Shelby confided. "And there was a rumor that he actually led a group of mercs down into Mexico to rescue Gracie Pendleton when she was kidnapped by that deposed South American dictator, Emilio Machado."

"I've heard about him," Morie said. She frowned. "Wasn't something said about a connection between Machado and our Rick Marquez, who works as a homicide detective with San Antonio P.D.?" she added.

"Yes," Tenny replied in a soft tone. "Some document has surfaced that connects him with Marquez's mother."

"Barbara, who owns the café in Jacobsville," Morie commented. "She has wonderful food. I've eaten there when I visited a girlfriend. . . ."

"No," Tenny interrupted gently. "Not his foster mother. His real mother."

Both women looked at her without speaking.

"Now isn't that interesting," Shelby said.

"And don't you dare repeat it," Tenny replied. "I heard it from someone I know and trust and I'm not supposed to tell. But you can keep a secret." She smiled as she met Shelby's eyes. "As I well know."

"Yes." Shelby didn't comment further, leaving her daughter to wonder about the strange remark.

Daryl came over to talk to King about a new seed bull that his father wanted to add to the breeding program, but he stopped by long enough to speak with Morie privately.

"You said you wanted rubies," he reminded her.

She flushed, because she hadn't

really taken the engagement thing seriously. He had, apparently. "Daryl . . ."

"If you don't like the design, we can change it," he assured her. He opened the jeweler's box. "I had it made up like this, because I know how much you love roses."

She caught her breath when she saw the rings. They were the most unique and beautiful settings she'd ever seen in her life. They looked like living blood in their exquisite eighteen-karat-gold settings. The engagement ring was a rose, its petals outlined in gold and set in glittering pigeon's blood rubies, the largest of which made the center. The engagement ring was studded with rubies and made to interlock with the wedding band.

"Here." Daryl pulled them out of the box and took her hand. He hesitated with a grin. "Want to try them on? No sales pressure. They come with a demented fiancé, but you can dump him anytime you like if you find someone more deserving."

She looked into his black eyes with real pleasure. He'd taken her to movies and taught her to tango, he'd ridden with her over the acres and acres of her father's huge ranch. He'd been a friend and even a confidant. She'd told him, although not her parents, the whole truth of her sojourn on the Rancho Real and found him a sympathetic and caring listener. He was also as quiet as a clam. He'd never divulged her secrets to her parents.

She could do worse.

He laughed, because she'd said it out loud. "Yes, you could," he assured her. "I even still have most of my own teeth!"

"Most of them?" she asked with a curious frown.

His black eyes twinkled. "Your brother knocked one of them out when we were in college together. I can't even remember what we fought over. But he said that since he couldn't beat me in a fair fight, we'd be better off as friends, and we have been, all these years."

"Yes, well, my brother has an attitude problem from time to time," she conceded. He was hot-tempered, the way Shelby had said their father once was, and he tended to be impulsive to a fault. But he was a good person. Like Daryl.

She shrugged. "Might as well try them on, since you went to so much trouble having them designed for me," she teased and held out her hand.

They were a perfect fit. They complemented her beautiful hands with their faint olive tan, and the settings glittered in the light with a thousand reflections. The cut was exquisite.

"I love them," she confessed.

He smiled. "Good! So. When are we getting married?"

She stared at him in panic. Mallory was still out there somewhere, even if he hated her and considered her a thief. She should hate him, but she couldn't. She loved him. The thing was, if he'd had second thoughts about her, he'd have been in touch by now. He'd have phoned, written, something, anything. But there had been only silence from him. He still thought she was a thief. It tormented her.

"He won't change his mind, Morena," he said gently, using her real name.

"Men like that are never wrong, in their own opinion. You're clinging to dreams. It's better, always better, to deal in reality."

"You're right, of course," she said in a subdued tone. "It's just . . ."

He bent and kissed her forehead. "An engagement isn't a marriage. Just say yes. We'll announce it at the production sale and make your father and my father very happy so they'll shut up trying to pressure us into getting married." He lifted his head. "And if things do somehow work out for you and your suspicious rancher, I'll take back the rings and go shopping elsewhere," he offered firmly. "You have nothing to lose, really."

She drew in a soft breath. He made sense. She didn't really agree, but she was certain that the future would be dark enough if she went through it alone. In some ways Daryl was perfect for her, and her father would be ecstatic. It might be enough to stop him from digging into her recent past and steamrolling over the Kirks in revenge if he found out why Mallory had fired her.

That alone was reason enough to say yes. Daryl was right about one other thing—an engagement wasn't a marriage. She could break it anytime she liked, with no hard feelings.

She touched the rings. "Pity to waste them."

"Just what I was thinking," he agreed.

Her dark eyes twinkled. "Okay. We can be engaged. But it's like a trial engagement," she added firmly. "Just that."

He touched her nose with the tip of his forefinger. "Just that. I promise."

Her father was over the moon when they gave him the news. "Thank God you finally saw sense," he told her. He shook Daryl's hand. "Welcome to the family. You can be married very soon."

"We're not rushing it," Daryl said, when he noted her discomfort. "We're going to take our time and get to know each other."

King's dark eyes narrowed. "Is that necessary? Why?"

"Now, Dad," Morie said gently. "Don't push."

"It's because of that damned Wyoming rancher who fired you, isn't it?" her father demanded suddenly. "The lowlife son of Satan is going to find himself on the wrong side of a defamation-of-character lawsuit just as soon as I find out who framed you! And his isn't the only head that's going to roll when I do!"

CHAPTER TEN

Morie felt her heart turn over at the anger and threat in her father's deep voice. "How did you . . . ?" she exclaimed, horrified that he was going to try to ruin the Kirks. They were in a precarious financial situation. He could do it.

"I didn't buy that story that you came home voluntarily. I know you," he returned curtly. "You were devastated by whatever happened. I had a friend in Houston do some digging. My, my, what I found out," he added softly, although his eyes were glittering.

She went closer to him. "Words," she said quietly. "It was all just words. I was set up . . . you know that. Mallory Kirk has a jealous girlfriend. She thought I was getting too close to him so she found a way to get me fired."

"You should have made him prose-cute you," King returned hotly. "I'd have had that blonde wannabe tied up in knots on the witness stand."

Witness stand. Jury. Her eyes nar-rowed. "You talked to Uncle Danny. He sold me out!"

He looked uncomfortable. "Danny didn't say anything. He just made some odd comments and I got suspicious about why you suddenly left a job you told him you loved."

"So you hired a private detective," she said with resignation. "Listen, Dad, it doesn't matter. I'm going to marry Daryl. Nobody knows me in Wyoming. Who cares what gossip goes around about why I left the ranch up there?"

"I care," he said flatly. "You're my child. You were accused of a crime. And now there's another crime that they may try to blame you for."

"Excuse me?" she asked, and her stomach flipped.

"A priceless jeweled egg was stolen from the house, and replaced with a cheap copy that went unnoticed until a few days ago," King said icily. "If they thought you stole it in the first place, they may come after you and have you prosecuted now that it's gone missing for real."

She felt sick. "I saw Mallory Kirk going back toward the house with it, just after he told me to leave."

"Yes, well, somebody took it soon afterward."

"I'd already left Wyoming," she protested.

"They could say you took it with you," he returned. "They could say you let Kirk find it in your rucksack because you had the real one hidden. It was an unsettling confrontation. He could say that he didn't notice it was a copy because of the emotional upset."

She sat down on the arm of the sofa, her expression tense and worried.

"I'm not about to let my daughter be labeled a thief," he said icily. "Your name is going to be cleared, and I don't care who else gets hurt. People who steal should be caught, Morena. You should have made them call the law and prosecute you."

"That's what Joe Bascomb did," she said bitterly. "And he was convicted of a murder, when he was innocent."

"Was he?" King asked, with narrowed yes. "Danny thinks there may be more to that story than you're aware of. He's the one who called in private detectives in the first place, to check out your friend Bascomb because you asked him for help, to get the man an attorney. In the process, they learned about the theft of the jeweled egg."

She felt even more terrible. Surely it couldn't get any worse. Could it?

She took a long breath. "Okay, you're right. But can it wait until after the production sale?" she asked gently. "Let's not spoil it with a lot of legal challenges. Mom's worked so hard."

King grimaced. He knew how hard Shelby had worked. She was the heart of the outfit, in many ways. "All right," he agreed after a minute. "That's only a few days away. But afterward," he added with ice in his tones, "we're going to set things straight in Wyoming."

She nodded. She wasn't looking forward to it. Mallory Kirk was in for a huge surprise, and not one he was going to enjoy. Her father would have him for breakfast. She studied her parent while he talked to Daryl. Under other circumstances, he might have liked Mallory. They were very similar in many ways. And hadn't her father been suspicious of Shelby and thought her an opportunist during their stormy relationship? He really didn't have much room to talk. Not that she was going to say that out loud.

Uncle Danny and his vivacious wife, Edie, came with their sons, and their housekeeper/cook, Safie, to stay during the production sale. Morie and Daryl took the kids riding and to movies to keep them occupied while the adults got everything organized for the sale.

The house was huge, and additions had been constructed while the kids

were in school so that they had entertainment areas for their friends. There
was an immense ballroom, an indoor
swimming pool, a tennis court out back,
the stables and a barn for King's prize
bulls. It was a lavish estate. Six Jag-
uars, two sedans, two convertibles and
two antique sports cars graced the ga-
rage. Cort and Morie owned the convertibles, although it had taken a long
time to convince King that they were as
safe as most other cars.

The Saturday morning that kicked off
the production sale came with a sud-
denness that Morie hadn't anticipated.
The small airport just south of the ranch
was kept busy as corporate jets landed,
refueled and took off again after de-
positing their passengers.

Morie was fascinated by the guest
list. She watched famous people stroll
around the premises with starstruck
awe.

"Stop that," Daryl teased, holding her
hand. "You've seen them before."

"Yes, on television," she assured him.

"Dad's never gone whole hog like this for a production sale!"

"He's making a statement," Daryl said in an odd tone.

She frowned. "Excuse me?"

He sighed. "Never mind." He grinned. "Race you to the sale barn!"

"I can't," she objected. "I have to help in the kitchen, making canapés. Even with all of us helping, including Aunt Edie and Safie and the caterers, it's a pinch getting it done in time for the party tonight. While all the visiting cattlemen are drooling over Dad's seed bulls, the women are grinding their teeth trying to provide enough food. And that doesn't include the barbecue that's going on in the tents for lunch," she added, indicating the row of tents and the smokers that were going full tilt to provide barbecue. "At least the cowboys are handling that for us! Thank goodness we got old Rafe to come out of retirement long enough to make those famous Dutch-oven biscuits he's famous for. Not to mention his beef barbecue."

"It will be worth it if your dad sells enough bulls," Daryl observed.

She thought of something. "Daryl, you have oil holdings. Do you do fracking?"

He glared at her. "No. We do offshore drilling, and we have a few rigs set up in Oklahoma, but we're very careful where we drill and we have safeguards in place. We have a wonderful record for safety."

"I didn't mean to offend," she said quickly. "But I wondered if you knew any companies that do fracking up in Wyoming."

"I know one that's trying to," he said. "A man named Cardman owns it. He's been sued in two states for lax safety procedures—if it isn't done properly, it contaminates the local water table. See, you inject water, and chemicals, at high pressure into the ground to fracture the shale rock and release oil and gas. It's not popular at the moment. There was even a documentary made about the dangers. That's one reason we don't invest in it."

"Cardman," she mused.

"He's a shady character," he affirmed. "He's known for buying up scrubland from unsuspecting landowners and then putting up operations on it. Several people have sued him. He just moves to another state and keeps going."

"Shame."

"Really."

She mentioned it to her mother when they were loading the last silver tray with hors d'oeuvres that evening, just before the guests congregated in the ballroom.

"Fracking," her mother mused. "What a nasty sort of operation it sounds."

"I know we need oil. Nobody wants to live in grass huts and walk fifty miles to a city," Morie stated. "But there are safe ways to extract oil, and then there's this high-speed injection fracturing. That woman I told you about kept trying to get Mallory to sell her friend some scrubland on his property. She didn't say why, but now I'm curious."

"You should mention it to your uncle Danny. He knows the Kirks."

"I might do that."

Shelby touched her daughter's cheek. The scratch had healed, and the skin was soft and velvety and blemishless, just like her own. "Sweetheart, are you really going to marry Daryl?"

"Dad wants me to."

"What do you want to do, Morena?"

Her dark eyes were sad. "I want to marry for love," she replied. "But when it isn't returned, maybe it's best to settle for someone honest and kind that you really like. Daryl is a wonderful person."

"He truly is. But if you don't love him, and he doesn't love you, the two of you are cheating each other." Her face was solemn. "I married for love. I've never regretted it. Not once."

"You were lucky," Morie said with a smile.

"Eventually." Shelby chuckled. "Oh, if you'd known your father as he used to be!" She rolled her eyes. "It was like domesticating a wolf!"

"It was?" Morie laughed.

"Worse! A grizzly bear." She pursed her perfect lips. "Your Mallory Kirk sounds just like your father. They'd butt heads at first, but then they'd be friends."

"Chance would be a fine thing." Morie sighed.

"I don't know. Life is funny," Shelby replied. "You never know what surprises are in store for you."

Fifteen minutes later, Morie had reason to remember that odd statement. Mallory Kirk walked in the door with Gelly Bruner.

Morie, standing beside Daryl, watched them come in with cold eyes. Her heart was cutting circles in her chest, but she was trying to act normally. In her exquisite white couture gown, with its thin strip of gold trim, and her long hair in an elegant upswept hairdo, dripping diamonds, she was the epitome of the wealthy debutante. Gelly was dressed in last year's fashion, again, a black dress that was passable but nothing to stir comment. Mallory, in evening dress, was impressive even if he didn't have movie-star looks. His tall, fit body was made for evening clothes. He looked elegant, if somber.

Morie saw her father moving toward Mallory with a sinking feeling in her stomach.

"You must be Kingston Brannt," Mallory said, extending a hand. "I'm Mallory Kirk. My brothers and I have a ranch in Wyoming. I came to get one of those seed bulls I've read so much about in cattle journals."

King didn't extend his own hand. He looked at the other man with black eyes that could have cut diamond. "I know who you are."

Mallory seemed puzzled. "This is my friend, Gelly Bruner."

"Mr. Brannt, I've heard so much about you," she purred.

King didn't even look at her.

"I've never seen so many famous people," Gelly was gushing. "You must know all the rich people on earth!"

"They're friends, Miss Bruner," King said curtly. "I don't choose them for their bank balances."

"Of course not," she said quickly.

"Hello, there," Danny Brant said to

Mallory, and he did shake hands. "How are your brothers?"

"Working, as usual. Good to see you again."

"Same here." He glanced at his brother, who was still seething. "We're always happy to have fellow cattlemen visit."

"I can't get over the decorations," Gelly enthused. "I'd love to know where you found so many antique roses!"

"Oh, that would be my niece. She's crazy about them," Danny said easily. "Her fiancé had a set of rings made for her with the design. There she is! Come over here, honey."

He was setting the cat among the pigeons and grinning. King was irritated that his brother had stolen his thunder, because he'd had something else in mind for the introduction.

Morie clung to Daryl's big hand as she joined them.

"This is my niece, Morena," Danny introduced. "And her fiancé, Daryl Coleman. He's CEO of an oil corporation."

Morena lifted her head proudly. She was aware of Gelly's suddenly white face, and Mallory's utter stillness as he registered who she was.

"Yes, my daughter worked for you for several weeks, I believe," King said in a voice that promised retribution. "And was allowed to quit rather than be prosecuted for theft. It might interest you to know that I've retained a private detective to investigate those charges. And I assure you," he growled, "countercharges will be forthcoming. Nobody accuses my daughter of being a damned thief!"

Mallory gaped at her. This elegant young woman, dressed in couture, living in luxury, engaged to be married, was the same ragged little cowgirl who'd turned his life upside down and left under a cloud of suspicion.

"Well . . . well, what a surprise," Gelly managed with a nervous laugh.

"Isn't it?" Morie asked. "By the way, Ms. Bruner, that friend of yours who wanted to buy the scrubland on the ranch, his name wouldn't be Cardman, by any chance, would it? Because Daryl has had some very interesting things to say about his past, and the lawsuits he's facing in several states for unsafe drilling practices."

"It was Cardman," Mallory replied, and stared at Gelly blankly. He'd had one too many surprises for one night.

"You should sell him the land," Morie advised with a pleasant smile. "Then when you want to see fireworks, all you'll have to do is set a match to your water."

He glared at her. "You lied," he said in a rasping tone.

"Well, thieves do lie, don't they?" she shot back.

He looked uncomfortable.

"My daughter is no thief," King told Mallory with glittering eyes. "She has no need to steal. I understand a priceless jeweled egg is missing from your ranch. Since my daughter seems to be involved in the case, I've hired Dane Lassiter out of Houston to investigate the theft for me."

"Cane hired him to investigate it for us," Mallory said stiffly. "And I don't think Morie took it," he added without meeting her eyes. "It was stolen after she left the ranch."

"How kind of you to move me off the suspect list," she said. "A few weeks late, of course." She was looking at Gelly, who was pale and unsteady on her feet. "Perhaps in the future, you'll be more careful about whom you set up for a burglary charge, Ms. Bruner. This one seems to have backfired on you."

"I didn't set anybody up," Gelly muttered. She pressed close to Mallory. "Could we leave? I won't be harassed like this!"

"You didn't mind harassing me, as I recall," Morie replied. "Or that poor cowboy who was fired for a missing drill that conveniently turned up in his suitcase."

"We need to go!" Gelly said. She was sounding hysterical.

"If you have any part in the charges against my daughter, Miss Bruner," King continued, staring straight at Gelly, "I will have my attorneys nail you to a wall. That's a promise. If you have one skeleton in your closet, I promise you'll see it on the evening news!"

Gelly let go of Mallory's arm and literally ran for the front door.

"As for you," King told Mallory Kirk, "in the history of this ranch, I have never had anyone escorted off the property. But if you and your 'friend' aren't gone within the hour, I swear to God I'll have the local sheriff escort you personally to the airport!"

Mallory sighed heavily. He looked at Morie, so beautiful in her gown, with her face taut and her eyes hard. She clung to that damned handsome kid, her fiancé, and looked as if it would make her happy never to see Mallory Kirk again as long as she lived. And he was dying for her. He'd missed her, wanted her, blamed himself for her condition. He'd imagined her ragged and poor, in a shelter somewhere because she couldn't find another job. And here she turned up in a mansion, surrounded by wealth, pampered by her father, the richest cattleman in Texas!

He'd been taken in by Gelly, lock, stock and barrel. Morie hated him. Her father hated him. He'd never live this down. He'd been stupid and judgmental, and he was getting just what he deserved. Morie had wanted to love him. He'd slapped her down. Now she was engaged to some other man, set to marry and start a family. Mallory would go back to Wyoming alone to reflect on his idiocy and face the future all by himself.

He stuck his big hands in his slacks pockets. "Well, if I had hemlock, I guess I'd drink it about now," he mused.

Danny muffled a laugh. Nobody else was amused. King looked murderous. Morie was impassive, on the surface at least.

In the middle of the confrontation, Shelby arrived. She lifted her eyebrows at the tableau. "My goodness, are we hosting a murder?" she mused.

Mallory looked at her with sudden recognition. "I know your face," he said gently.

She smiled. "I was a professional model when I married King," she said, sliding her hand through King's arm.

"Your mother was Maria Kane, the actress," Mallory continued. She nodded.

"I've been watching her old movies on late-night television," he commented. He glanced at Morie. "Now I know why you looked so familiar to us."

"She favors my mother," Shelby replied. "Mr. . . . ?"

"Kirk. Mallory Kirk."

The smile immediately left Shelby's elfin face. Her dark eyes began to glitter.

Mallory sighed. "No need for further introductions." He nodded and glanced down at Morie. "For the record, nobody thought you took the damned egg. You had no opportunity. As for the charge I made, I apologize. I've been blind, deaf, dumb and stupid, as my brothers have reminded me every hour on the hour since you left. I guess it took a kick in the head to convince me." He shrugged. "I don't need a road map to see which direction I need to look for a thief." His face set in hard lines. "I'm genuinely sorry," he told the Brannts. "She was one of the hardest-working hires I've ever had. Never complained. Never fussed. Never asked for concessions or special treatment and took risks that

I'd never have let her take if I'd known about them."

Morie didn't speak. She was too sick at heart. It was too late. Much too late.

"What risks?" King asked coldly.

"For one, a confrontation with an escaped convicted killer who's a friend of my brother Tank," he replied.

"He isn't guilty," Morie said defensively. "I'm sure of it."

"And I'm sure that he is," Mallory replied. "Tank's fond of him and he won't listen to reason." He glanced wryly at King, who was still smoldering. "Family character trait, I'm afraid. But the fact is, Joe Bascomb has an atrocious temper and he once beat a mule almost to death. Any man who'll treat livestock like that will treat a man like that."

"Nobody treats animals that way here," King said.

"Or on my place," Mallory agreed.

"You should let him stay," Danny told King.

King smiled. It wasn't a nice smile. "He won't like it here."

Mallory glanced at Morie's stiff little face and he felt a cold, hollow place inside him. "You might have just told me who you were in the first place."

"I wanted to learn ranch work and he—" she nodded toward her father "—wouldn't let me near it."

"You were raised to be a lady," King said curtly. "Not a cowhand."

"You had no business lifting heavy limbs off fences!" Mallory agreed hotly.

"Don't yell at my daughter," King said angrily.

"Your daughter was an idiot," Mallory shot back. "She could have ruined her health. I thought she was what she claimed to be, a poor girl down on her luck who needed a job desperately!"

"I did need a job," Morie said defensively. "I got sick and tired of men wanting me for what my father had instead of what I was!"

Mallory glared at Daryl.

Daryl grinned at him. "Wrong number," he said defensively. "My folks are on the Fortune 500 list, and I have my own very successful businesses. I don't need to marry money."

"He had the same problem," Morie

replied. "That's why we're marrying each other."

"Not true," Daryl replied.

She gaped at him. "Not true?"

"She's marrying me because I can do the tango," Daryl said easily, and smiled down at her.

She shifted restlessly. "Well, yes. Most men can't dance." She looked pointedly at her father.

"Your mother didn't marry me for my dancing skills," King pointed out.

"Good thing," Shelby agreed, and she seemed to unbend just a little. She looked past Mallory. "I believe your friend is motioning to you."

He turned. Gelly was making frantic motions toward the door.

"She's just afraid that she'll be arrested before you can get her to an airplane," Morie said with a pleasant smile. The smile faded. "And that might be the truth."

Mallory felt like an insect under a magnifying glass. He knew he wasn't going to change minds or win hearts here, not in this atmosphere. He'd have to go back home and do what he could to undo the damage. Morie was going to marry that handsome yahoo, was she? Not if he could help it.

"Don't you marry him," he told her firmly, nodding toward Daryl.

"Well, you can't tango," she said sourly.

"How do you know?" he replied.

"He isn't staying long enough to demonstrate any dancing skills," King said impatiently.

"I'm going." Mallory turned away. But he hesitated. "We all make mistakes. It's why they put erasers on pencils."

"Some of us make bigger mistakes than others," Morie replied. "I'll concede that I shouldn't have applied for work without telling you the truth. But you should have given me the benefit of the doubt," she added coldly.

"Under the circumstances, that didn't seem possible."

"Not with your girlfriend planting evidence right and left," Morie replied curtly.

"Not my girlfriend," Mallory said quietly. "Not anymore." He looked right into Morie's eyes as he said it, and her whole body tingled.

"I'm getting married," Morie informed him with a tight smile. "So don't look at me to replace her."

"Fat chance," Mallory said with a glance at a glowering Kingston Brannt. "I'll be damned if I'll marry into any family he belongs to."

"That goes double for my daughter!" King snapped.

Mallory looked at Shelby and shook his head. "You must be one gutsy lady."

"Because I married him?" Shelby managed a smile. "He's not so bad, once you get to know him."

"Which you won't," King muttered. "Aren't you leaving?"

"I guess I am," Mallory agreed. He glanced at Morie again with faint pride and obvious regret. "You wouldn't like to hear my side of it?"

"Sure," she replied. "Just like you wanted to hear my side of it."

He glanced from one family member to another, turned and walked slowly away. Gelly grabbed his arm at the front door and started talking before they even got halfway out it. But Mallory wasn't listening.

*   *   *

"Well, I can see why you had to leave Wyoming," Shelby said after the guests had gone home and they were sitting on Morie's bed.

"He's a pain," Morie agreed. "But did you see the look on Gelly's face when she realized who I was?" she mused. "It did my heart good."

"She's probably realized how much trouble she's going to be in, as well," Shelby replied. She studied her daughter's face. "You really love that man, don't you?"

Morie closed up like a sensitive plant at sundown. "I thought I did," she replied. "But if he could take someone else's word for my character, he doesn't know me. He doesn't want to know me. He's happy living as a bachelor with his brothers."

"I wonder."

"I lived in dreams," Morie said, fingering the expensive comforter. "I thought he was getting to know me and enjoying it, as I was. I thought he wanted me. All the time, he was just playing."

"Why would he do that?" Shelby wondered aloud. "He doesn't seem a frivolous man."

Morie blinked. "He isn't."

"Perhaps he's been hunted for his wealth, too."

"He's still being hunted for it, or didn't you notice Gelly?" Morie laughed.

"A woman with an eye to the main chance, and quite cold-blooded, if you ask me," Shelby agreed.

"Even his brothers suspected she was setting me up, but Mallory wouldn't listen. He's bullheaded to a fault!"

"Just like your father, dear."

"I guess so."

"You shouldn't marry Daryl when you're still in love with another man," Shelby said abruptly. "It's not fair to either of them."

Morie didn't answer. She was remembering the shock on Mallory's face when he saw her in the beautiful gown, holding Daryl's hand. It had been sweet vengeance. But it was a long step from that to forgiveness.

"How could I ever trust him again?" Morie wondered aloud. "Who's to say that he wouldn't do the same thing twice?"

Shelby kissed her cheek. "Love requires trust. Now I'm going to bed. We'll talk some more tomorrow, okay? I'm very tired."

"I know you are. Everything went perfectly. Well, except for Mallory walking in and spoiling the evening."

"He held his own against your father, you know," Shelby murmured drily. "That's not easy. Most other men are terrified of him. Mallory wasn't."

Morie had noticed that. It made her proud. But she wasn't going to say it.

"Sleep well," she told her mother, and hugged her tight.

Shelby kissed her dark hair. "You, too, my darling. Good night."

CHAPTER ELEVEN

"You can't believe them!" Gelly exclaimed, almost hysterically. "She's rich, so she can accuse me of things and I can't defend myself!"

He glanced at Gelly in the seat of the corporate jet beside him. "Weren't you just on the other end of that argument?"

She glowered at him. "She stole the egg. I know she did. You saw it in her bag!"

"I did, didn't I?" He was still kicking himself mentally for believing Morie guilty in the first place.

"I did not plant it there. I swear!"

"They've hired a private detective. So have my brothers. The same detective—how's that for a coincidence?" he murmured.

She shifted in her seat. This was getting too close for comfort. She couldn't endure a thorough background check. "I'll sue for invasion of privacy!"

"Gelly, the detective is investigating the theft of a priceless jeweled egg," he reminded her. "How does that involve your privacy?"

She cleared her throat. "I'm sorry." She forced a smile. "I wasn't thinking clearly. I'm very upset. Her father is obnoxious!"

"He loves her. He's very protective. I'd be that way about my own kids."

She snuggled up to him. "Wouldn't you like to have a family? I would. We could get married right away."

"We could. But we aren't going to."

"But you like me, don't you?"

He looked down into eyes like cash registers, as cold as ice, and realized that he'd never seen Gelly as she really was until now. It had taken a near tragedy to open his eyes to her real nature.

"You really want to be rich, don't you?"

She gaped at him. "Who doesn't?"

"There are things more important than money."

She laughed coldly. "Of course there are, if you've got it."

"I want to hear more about that friend of yours, Cardman," he said suddenly.

She looked around restlessly. "He's just someone I know. He's down on his luck."

"Would it be because of the lawsuits?"

She cleared her throat. "I think I'll try to have a little nap," she said with a practiced smile. "I've had a very upsetting evening. You don't mind?"

"I don't mind."

She curled up in her seat and pillowed her head on her arm. Mallory got up and went to sit in the front seat, where he had access to a laptop. He opened it and started doing some digging of his own.

* * *

When he got home, his brothers were both in the living room, having coffee and watching the news before bedtime.

They stared at him curiously. "You're back early," Tank said. "I thought the plan was to fly back in tomorrow."

"There was an unexpected surprise."

They both raised eyebrows.

Mallory stuck both hands in the pockets of his dress slacks and glared at them. "Kingston Brannt has a daughter."

"Oh?" Cane mused with a wicked smile.

"Does he, now?" Tank added. "And you noticed her?"

"It was hard not to," Mallory snapped. "She worked for us for several weeks."

There were shocked faces all around.

"Morie?" Cane asked. "She's the daughter of that Brannt?"

"Told you the name wasn't a coincidence, didn't I?" Tank mused. "She had quality and breeding."

"What the hell was she doing working for wages?" Cane wanted to know.

"She got tired of men wanting to

marry her for her money," Mallory said tersely.

"I can understand that," Tank agreed.

"So she found a man who was loaded and now she's engaged to him," Mallory continued in a dull tone. "He's a pretty boy. His father's in the Fortune 500. No gold digging there. And her father likes *him.*"

It was the emphasis on the last word that caught their attention.

"King doesn't like you, I'm assuming," Cane mused.

"Fat chance. I accused his daughter of theft and fired her," Mallory said heavily. He took off his jacket, loosened his tie and dropped down into his recliner. "I must have been blind, to think she'd steal from us."

"You had Gelly helping you think it," Cane said sourly.

"Gelly was half-hysterical when we left," Mallory confided. "Morie's father hired a private detective." He glanced at Cane. "The same one you hired, Dane Lassiter. When he mentioned that, Gelly almost fainted. And there's something else. That friend of hers,

Cardman, who wanted to buy our scrubland, he's in the oil business. He does the fracturing process with injection wells to extract oil. He's being sued in several states for sloppy work that resulted in groundwater contamination."

"I seem to recall that you were in favor of selling him that land," Tank commented to Mallory.

"Go ahead, rub it in. I've been a complete idiot," Mallory grumbled. "No need to feel shy about commenting."

"Anybody can be fooled by a woman," Cane said sourly.

"Except me," Tank said with a grin.

Nobody said anything. It wasn't true. He used to have a fail-safe radar when it came to women. In fact, he'd been the first to suspect that Gelly wasn't what she seemed to be. But his own track record was blemished since his last failed romance.

"What about Morie?" Cane asked.

"What about her?" Mallory returned belligerently.

"Don't try to fool us . . . we're your family," Tank replied. "It was obvious that you felt something for her, even if you were fighting it tooth and nail."

Mallory's dark eyes grew narrow. "Maybe I did. But I'm not marrying into any family that belongs to King Brannt!"

"Ooooh," Tank murmured drily. "Venomous."

"Absolutely," Cane agreed.

"He's bullheaded, uncompromising, acid-tongued, confrontational, bad-tempered and he has the parlor manners of a rabid moose!"

"So you liked him, then," Cane replied, nodding and smiling.

"I've never seen a rabid moose," Tank commented.

"I'll fly you to Texas. You can see for yourself," Mallory muttered.

"To give the man credit, it would be offensive to have his only daughter charged with theft. And from what I've heard, nobody has a temper the equal of King Brannt's."

"I gather that you didn't get to meet Cort at the party?" Cane mused.

Mallory frowned. "Who's Cort?"

"Her older brother. If you think King's got a temper, you ain't seen nothing yet," Cane drawled. "A cattleman made a nasty remark about his conservation practices that he didn't like and he put the man through an antique screen in a restaurant. Police came, arrests were made. Cort just laughed. The cattleman was selling supposedly purebred cattle with bloodlines that were, shall we say, not of the purest. Cort exposed him at the hearing. The charges were dropped, very quickly, and the cattleman did a disappearing act. I hear they're still looking for him."

"Any cattleman worth his salt can spot a good bull by conformation alone," Tank scoffed.

"Yes, well, the cattleman was selling his stock to a newcomer from back east who'd just bought a ranch and was buying bulls for his new herd," he replied. "He was furious when he found out what he'd lost."

"God help us," Tank exclaimed. "So the perp skipped and left his pigeon holding the bag. Tragic."

"Perp? You still talk like a lawman," Cane remarked.

Tank shrugged. It was painful to remember how he'd been shot up during the border incident. But it was getting easier to live with.

"Sorry," Cane said gently. "I wasn't trying to bring back bad memories. I forget sometimes."

Tank smiled. "Me, too. No problem."

Mallory was listening, but not commenting. He was seeing Morie in her beautiful gown, her black hair upswept, her creamy shoulders on view. He was seeing that handsome yahoo holding her waist and feeling the anger rise in him at the sight. She'd been his, if he'd wanted her. He'd kissed her, held her, touched her. She was innocent. Was she still? Or had she gone rushing into that playboy's bed, full of grief and anguish at Mallory's rejection and distrust?

"Damned pretty boy," Mallory muttered to himself.

"Excuse me?" Cane replied.

"Morie's fiancé," he said coldly.

"I'm sure that she only likes him because he's handsome," Tank said with a wry glance at his brother.

"You can talk," Mallory said irritably.

"Both of you got the looks in the family. I favor our grandfather, God help me. He looked like his face caught fire and somebody put it out with an ax."

They both practically rolled on the floor laughing.

"Well, we're still stuck with lawsuits drifting in," Mallory said heavily. "Brannt's going to sue us for defamation of character."

"He won't," Cane replied easily. "Morie won't let him. She's got a heart."

"A big one," Tank agreed. "She's as innocent as Joe Bascomb."

Cane was silent. Mallory stared at him pointedly. "You're loyal to your friends. It's one of your finest traits. But Joe beat his father's mule senseless and almost killed it. Have you forgotten that?"

"Joe said it was his dad," Tank replied tautly.

"There were witnesses, Tank," Mallory said gently. "His mother was taken to the emergency room around the same time with a fractured arm. The talk was that she tried to stop Joe from beating the mule and he hit her with the tire iron."

"She said she fell," Tank replied doggedly.

"You don't want to hear these things, but you already know that Joe got out of the army on a mental," Cane reminded him. "He attacked two men in his barracks for making fun of him because he couldn't spell. Put one of them in the hospital."

"That might all be true, but he could still be innocent of deliberately causing the death of the man who was beating Laura Teasley."

"I know," Cane said. "But there's a pattern of violent behavior going back a long way. It came out at the trial. Besides that, Laura testified that Joe already had a grudge against the victim for a blacksmithing job he did and wasn't paid for."

"We were talking about the Brannts," Tank said, changing the subject abruptly. "And we still have the problem of who took that egg."

"The only people who had access to this room were Mavie—and we know she didn't do it—and us. And Gelly," Cane added quietly.

"That's not quite true, is it, Tank?" Mallory asked suddenly, and with a pointed stare.

Tank glared at him. "Joe was only in here once, just before he was arrested," he said.

"Tank, he came on the place without even being noticed when he approached Morie at the line cabin," Mallory reminded him. "He's a woodsman. He can get into and out of anything. He's a locksmith, in addition to being a blacksmith. He can open locks."

"Isn't it enough that he's being accused of a murder he didn't commit? Do we have to start accusing him of theft, as well?" Tank exclaimed, exasperated. He got up. "I'm going to bed. Arguing gets us nowhere."

"Me, too," Cane agreed. He got to his feet. "Dane Lassiter has one of his best detectives up here poking around. He'll dig up something. I'm sure of it."

"Most of it will probably concern Gelly, I'm afraid," Tank said with a worried look at Mallory. "I hope you aren't more involved with her than you seem to be."

"I'm not," Mallory said heavily. "She was just somebody to take around places."

"You'd better hope she doesn't come up with a better accusation than the ones she made against Morie and our former cowhand," Cane told him.

"Like what?" Mallory asked, stunned.

"Maybe she'll turn up pregnant," Cane said.

Mallory's dark eyes twinkled. "Not by me," he said. "I'm not that careless."

"She could lie."

"Bloodwork would exonerate me," Mallory said easily. "I was never intimate with her in the first place."

"Good thing," Tank said.

"Yes," Cane agreed.

Mallory didn't mention that there had been a close call once, just once, after Morie left and he was depressed enough to need comforting. But he hadn't crossed the line with Gelly. So even if she made the charge, he'd be able to refute it. He did worry, though, that she might try to trap him. She wanted money and now she was desperate. He wondered if she might have taken that priceless egg. She did have the opportunity and the motive. It would have to wait for the private detective to iron it out, he supposed.

He went up to bed, his mind still full of Morie's real identity and the picture that he'd carry forever in his heart, of her in that white gown, looking as elegant as a princess and quite at home among the wealthiest cattlemen in the world.

A few days later, a tall, dark man with long black hair and pale gray eyes, wearing a suit, knocked at the front door.

Mavie let him in and called Mallory, who was the only brother in the house at the moment.

"Ty Harding." The man introduced himself and shook hands with Mallory. "I work for Dane Lassiter, out of Houston."

"Come in," Mallory invited. "Mavie, coffee?"

"Coming right up," she said, casting

a last, smiling glance at the handsome newcomer. Not only was he handsome, he had the physique of a movie star, tall and muscular without being overtly so.

Harding sat down across from Mallory. "I've finished the investigation."

"Then you know who took the egg?" Mallory asked at once.

He nodded grimly. "It was sold to a fence in Denver through a third party for ten thousand dollars."

Mallory gaped at him. "It's worth ten times that!"

"Yes, we know. The fence has been arrested and the egg was confiscated from its new owner. He's pretty upset. He paid a quarter of a million for it. Luckily, the fence hadn't had time to distribute more than a third of the money."

Mallory was relieved. "That piece of art was our grandmother's," he explained. "It really is priceless, but it has a sentimental value, as well. Who stole it?"

Harding hesitated. Mavie came in with steaming cups of black coffee in mugs on a silver tray. There was pound cake, too. She put it down, grinning at the newcomer. She didn't smile much. Mallory was amused at her friendliness to the visitor. "Hope you like cake," she said. "It was made fresh yesterday."

"I love it. Thank you."

"Cream? Sugar?" she offered.

Harding shook his head and chuckled, showing perfect white teeth. "I got used to drinking it black years ago. It's hard to find condiments in some of the places I've worked."

"Thank you, Mavie," Mallory said pointedly.

She glanced at him, cleared her throat, excused herself and left.

"Nice lady," Harding commented as he sipped coffee. He closed his eyes. "Colombian," he decided. "My favorite."

Mallory's eyes widened. "You can tell the origin of the blend?"

"It's a hobby." His eyes twinkled with secret amusement.

Mallory didn't comment. "Now. Who took the egg?"

Harding had another sip of coffee

and put the cup down. "A threesome, I'm afraid."

"What threesome?" Mallory's mind was working overtime as he searched for suspects.

"A local woman, Gelly Bruner, took the egg. She had a key to your cabinet, which was made for her by an escaped convict, Joe Bascomb, who needed money to avoid being captured. There was a third man involved, peripherally, a man named Bates. It seems he helped Ms. Bruner by planting evidence."

Mallory's face was thunderous. "Bates works for me! He said he saw Morie Brannt holding the egg in the bunkhouse."

"I believe he also helped plant evidence on another cowboy who worked here, a man named Harry Rogers, who's retained counsel and plans to sue for false arrest."

"Great," Mallory said. "I guess we'll keep our lawyers busy."

"Rogers does have a case, but it's the sheriff who arrested him that he's suing, and also Ms. Bruner. He isn't suing you. He said you were set up, just as he was."

Mallory was touched. "In that case he can have his job back with a raise, if he wants it, and I'll pay for his attorney."

"You'd have to talk to him about that. Your cowboy Bob Bates has been arrested, however, and charged with aiding and abetting theft."

"I'm just astonished," Mallory said heavily. "I did suspect Gelly, but I had no idea Bates was that involved."

"He had feelings for her and he's very young," Harding replied. "He's sick at heart about what he did. She told him it was a prank. He didn't find out different until Ms. Brannt was fired, and then he was afraid to come forward."

"It doesn't excuse theft," Mallory said. "Not at all."

"He's a first offender," Harding said. "I'm almost certain that he'll get probation. Ms. Bruner is, however, in a different situation. She has a record."

"For what?" Mallory asked, stunned.

"Theft. This isn't her first walk around the justice system. She's never been convicted, but she's been charged twice in the theft of priceless antiques from private homes. I'm afraid she's not going to have an easy time. Her signature was on the receipt for proceeds from the sale of the stolen egg, and Bates is turning state's evidence against her in return for first-offender status. He can put her in the house with a duplicate key at the time of the theft. It seems that Bascomb also made her a copy of your house key."

"Oh, good God," Mallory exclaimed.

"So it might be a good idea for you to check your other valuables and see if any are missing or have been replaced with copies," the detective suggested.

"I'll do that today," Mallory agreed. "That's a lot of good detective work for such a short time."

Harding shrugged. "I love my job. I used to be a cop, but I got tired of the hours, so I quit Houston P.D. and went to work for Dane Lassiter." He grinned. "He's some boss, let me tell you."

"So I've heard."

"There's a rumor going around that

Joe Bascomb didn't get his cut of the money and he's out for revenge," Harding added. "If I were you, I'd put on extra patrols out here and watch where I went. He's really desperate now. They've brought in other law-enforcement personnel to go into the woods after him, including some trackers and some K-9 units."

"I'll make sure we're all armed," Mallory told him. "And thanks."

Harding smiled. "My pleasure."

Mallory told his brothers what Harding had related, and they went around the house looking for other missing objects. To their shock, they found at least two priceless ceramic vases missing and one irreplaceable solid gold miniature goblet, not to mention an entire silver service that was kept apart from the others in a special cabinet. It was almost never unlocked and the brothers paid it little attention, because it was in an out-of-the-way place in the house.

Mallory called the sheriff's department and an officer took down the descriptions of the missing items and their value. He promised to have their investigator get in touch with the appropriate authorities in Denver and search for them. Mallory didn't expect them to be found. But there was always a chance, even if it was a small one.

Gelly had called him collect from the detention center, crying and begging for help. "I'm innocent," she wailed. "I'm being set up! It's a lie!"

"Gelly, you had duplicate keys that Bascomb made for you," he added. "The prosecutor has an eyewitness who saw you sell the jeweled egg to a dealer in Las Vegas. What do you expect me to do?"

"You have to help me!" she exclaimed. "I'll tell them I'm pregnant! I'll call the newspapers!"

"Go ahead," he said easily.

"I mean it!"

"So do I," he replied. "You'd have to prove it. We both know it's impossible."

"Well, I know that. But I can lie," she shot back. "I know how to lie and make people believe me!"

"You sure do," he agreed coldly. "You

got Morie fired with your lies. Not to mention Harry Rogers, who worked for us and was fired for stealing a drill that he didn't even take."

"That silly girl," Gelly muttered. "I made up all sorts of stories about her, and you believed every one of them!"

"Yes. I did," he replied grimly.

"Maybe I can't have you, but you'll never have her, now!" she exclaimed. "I can't imagine that she'd really want you. You're as ugly as an old boot!"

His pride ached at the charge. "Maybe," he replied coldly. "But I'm rich."

"Humph!"

"Goodbye, Gelly."

He hung up and removed the cartridge that had the conversation on it. Even though he hadn't informed her that she was being recorded, this would serve as evidence that he wasn't responsible for any pregnancy she might claim in the future. He dropped it in the drawer of the telephone table, replaced it with a new one and then blocked the number she'd called from—the detention center—so that she couldn't reach him again. Her words stung. He knew he had nothing in the looks department. He turned and went out to work. But his mind wasn't at all on what he was doing. Which was a shame.

Morie was walking around the barn with her father and brother. She hadn't said two words all morning.

Cort was tall like their father, with jet-black hair and eyes. He was drop-dead gorgeous, Morie thought, even if he was her brother. Now he glanced at her with narrowed eyes. "Don't be thinking about that damned Wyoming coyote," he said hotly. "He's not worth a single thought."

"Amen," King Brannt muttered.

"Neither of you know a thing about him," Morie replied without looking up. "He has good qualities. He was taken in by Gelly Bruner."

"His brothers weren't," King replied.

"Love blinds men," Morie said with more pain than she realized. "Mallory is in love with Gelly."

Both men looked down at her.

King, undemonstrative to a fault, nevertheless put his arm around his daughter and hugged her close. "Daryl will make you a good husband," he told her firmly.

She smiled. "I know."

"If she doesn't love him, he won't," Cort cut in bluntly.

King glared at his son. "You're supposed to be on my side."

"I am on your side. But she's my sister and I love her," the younger man added. "It's not a good idea to jump into a new relationship when you haven't resolved the old one."

"I never had a relationship with that awful cattleman," Morie muttered.

King let her go and searched her face. "Are you sure?"

"I'm sure," she said firmly.

King raised an eyebrow. "He was looking at you the way I look at a juicy steak when your mother's been feeding me chicken for a week."

Morie's heart jumped. "He was?"

King shrugged. "He stood up to me, too."

"I thought you didn't like him." Morie faltered.

"I heard from the private detective," he continued. "It seems Ms. Bruner is in jail awaiting trial on theft by taking, along with one of the Kirks' cowboys. That escaped criminal they're looking for is on the list, too, but they still can't find him."

"It was on the news this morning," Cort said. "They've sent in tracking dogs."

"I feel sorry for Tank," Morie said. "Joe Bascomb was his friend."

"Tank?" Cort asked, blinking.

"He killed one overseas and his men gave him the nickname," Morie volunteered.

Cort sighed. "I guess it's better than Tub."

Tub was what they called one of their cowboys, who was thin as a rail and the best wrangler they'd ever had. Nobody knew how he'd come by the nickname.

"They said that Bascomb had told a family member that he had a score to settle before he was caught, and that they wouldn't take him alive."

Morie felt cold chills run down her

arms. It was an odd sort of apprehension, as if she knew something terrible was about to happen and that she had no way of stopping it.

"I feel odd," she murmured.

"Odd, how?" her father asked.

Before she could answer, Shelby came into the barn, looking like a fashion plate even in jeans and a T-shirt. She was frowning.

"What's wrong, honey?" King asked, sensitive to her moods. He caught her by her arms, gently, smiling down at her. "Can I help?"

She shook her head and looked at Morie with sorrow. "It's about that cattleman you worked for, Mallory Kirk."

Morie's heart stopped, skipped and ran away. "What about him?"

"That escaped criminal kidnapped him on his own ranch. He says he's going to kill him . . . Morie!"

Morie didn't hear her. She'd fainted dead away.

CHAPTER TWELVE

If it disturbed her family that Morie fainted at the news that Mallory had been kidnapped, her next move horrified them. She announced plans to fly up to Wyoming.

"What in the world do you think you can do that the law can't?" King demanded hotly.

"I can talk to Joe Bascomb," she said flatly.

"Nobody can talk to him—he's desperate." Her brother tried to reason with her. "He might kidnap you and kill you, too."

"He won't," she said, certain of it. "I talked to him. I shared my lunch with him. He'll listen to me."

Shelby hadn't said anything yet. She was watching, listening, worrying.

"Mom, remember when old man Hughes got drunk?" she asked gently. "Remember who they'd call to come get him out of bars or fights? It was me. He'd always do what I asked, no matter how mad or mean he was."

"Yes, I remember," Shelby said. "You have a way with people."

"Joe Bascomb isn't going to listen to any man," she said quietly. "But he might listen to a woman."

King was grinding his teeth. "I won't let you risk it."

She went close to him. "Yes, you will, Dad," she said gently. "Because it's what you'd do, in my place, and you know it." Her eyes darkened. "I love Mallory Kirk. He may be gullible, and he may be a terror of a man, but I can't let him die and not try to save him."

King drew in a long breath. "I guess you can't."

She pulled off her engagement ring and put it in his hand. "Please give that back to Daryl and tell him I did find somebody better, but only because it's a man I love. He'll understand."

"He will," King agreed. "I'll have them fuel the jet."

"Thanks."

He kissed her forehead. "Don't get killed." He wasn't teasing.

"I won't. I promise." She hugged him and her brother and then her mother.

"I could go with you," Cort volunteered.

"They don't need any more troublemakers than they've already got up there," King mused, shaking his head at his son. "You're too much like me. You'd just put everybody's back up."

Cort shrugged, but he didn't dispute the assessment. He tugged at Morie's long black hair. "Be safe."

She nodded. "I will be. I promise."

She phoned Tank from the airport. He and Cane both came to get her. But when she explained what she wanted to do, they were adamantly against it.

"He'd listen to me if he'd listen to anybody," Tank argued. He was gaunt, like Cane. It had been a rough couple of days since Mallory went riding fence out near the old line cabin and didn't return. Joe Bascomb had phoned a few hours later and told them that he had Mallory and he was going to kill him for messing up his financial coup. Tank had pleaded with his friend, but Joe said he had nothing to lose and he wasn't talking to them again. He hung up.

"Mal may already be dead," Tank said heavily. "We have no way of knowing."

"I don't think he is," she said, without explaining why she thought that. She knew inside herself, knew certainly, that Mallory was still alive. She knew it.

"You don't even know how to find Joe, if we were to agree to let you try," Cane argued.

"I do know," she said. "I'll go to the line cabin and wait for him. He'll come. He watches it."

They frowned.

"That's where he took Mal from," Cane recalled. "We saw signs of a struggle."

"Why the cabin?" Tank wondered.

She gave them a droll look. "It's provisioned, isn't it? There's even a bed. And nobody stays out there except when there's a need. Where do you think he's been living all this time, in a cave?"

"You might have voiced that suspicion earlier," Tank muttered.

"I was having a little problem with credibility around here at the time," she said drily.

They looked upset.

"I know you two believed I was innocent," she said. "Thanks."

Cane studied her curiously. "Mallory said you sparkled like a jewel at your family ranch. Kingston Brannt's daughter, riding fence lines." He shook his head. "We could hardly believe it."

"Dad wouldn't let me near the cattle," she said, beaming inside at their description of what Mallory had said about her. "Neither would my brother.

And I was being forcefully courted for my father's money. I needed a break."

"Mallory's been kicking himself ever since he got home," Tank told her. "He thinks he's too ugly to appeal to a woman for himself, so all they want is his money."

"He's not ugly. Stupid, yes," she muttered. "Idiotic. Distrustful. Bad-tempered . . . !"

"We know all that," Cane acknowledged. "But we love him."

She glanced at them sadly. "Yes. So do I. It's why I came. And I won't be discouraged from doing this. I'm right."

"If Joe doesn't kill Mal," Tank said quietly, "and it works out that he lets him go, he'll kill us for letting you take the risk."

"We can deal with that when it happens. Right now, I need to change clothes, borrow a horse and ride out to the line cabin."

"It's pouring down rain," Cane said.

"No problem. I packed a raincoat!"

She'd also packed five thousand dollars in large bills, with which she was going to appeal to Joe to release Mallory. It was a calculated risk. He might grab her and the money, and kill her with Mallory. But she was willing to take the chance that he wouldn't. He was a basic sort of person. He needed money and he was angry that he'd been double-crossed. But he still needed money and he might bargain for it. The sheriff was closing in. He'd need to get out quickly. He wouldn't know that Morie had already spoken to the sheriff, who was another friend of Uncle Danny's, and outlined her plan. He would have two government agents in the woods overlooking the line cabin, woodsmen as good or better than Joe Bascomb. She couldn't tell the brothers that, in case they let something slip. So she kept her counsel.

Darby was upset when she had him saddle the horse for her.

"You can't do this," he protested as she loaded a small pouch, along with a bag of biscuits and a thermos of coffee that Mavie, protesting, too, had made for her to take along. "You can't let her do it!" he raged at the two brothers standing grimly nearby.

"Yes, they can, Darby," Morie told him gently. "I won't let Joe kill Mallory. No matter what I have to do to save him."

"It's not right."

She smiled. "Yes, it is. You just send up a prayer or two for me, okay?"

"Dozens," he promised grimly. "I wish I'd known who you were at the start. I'd never have let you go riding fence in the first place."

"If you hadn't, I wouldn't have gotten to know Joe Bascomb and I wouldn't have a prayer of convincing him to release Mallory. Things work the way they're supposed to. There's a plan, and a purpose, to everything," she said, shocking herself because she remembered saying that to Joe.

She mounted up gracefully and turned the gelding. Rain was peppering down over her slicker and wide-brimmed hat. It was getting dark, too, but she wouldn't let that deter her. She had a flashlight in her pack. "Try not to worry. I'll call you as soon as I know anything." She had a cell phone in the pocket of her slicker. She patted it.

"If we don't hear from you in an hour, we're coming in," Tank said quietly.

She nodded. "Fair enough."

She turned the horse again and galloped off toward the line cabin. All she had was hope. But hope was the very last thing anyone ever lost.

Morie pulled up at the line cabin and dismounted. She took the biscuits and thermos and money out of her saddlebag, along with her flashlight.

She noticed movement at the curtain. She'd guessed right. Joe was in that cabin. She wondered if he had Mallory there, and prayed that he did. If he'd already killed Mallory, her life would be worth nothing.

She went up the steps and opened the door. She looked down the barrel of a loaded shotgun.

"What are you doing here?" Joe Bascomb demanded hotly.

She felt sick at her stomach, and she was scared to death. But she didn't dare show it. She only smiled. "Brought you something."

He blinked. The gun wavered. "Brought me something?"

She nodded.

He hesitated. She glanced around the single room. Mallory wasn't there. Her heart sank. What if he was already dead?

The shotgun barrel lowered. "What did you bring?" he asked.

"Is Mallory Kirk alive?" she asked.

He drew in a long, worried breath. He stared at her.

"Is he alive?" she asked again, more unsteadily.

He put on the safety and laid the shotgun across the long, rough wooden table. "Yes," he said after an eternity of seconds.

She let out the breath she'd been holding. "Where is he?"

"Tied up against a tree, some distance from here," he said curtly. "Where he won't be found. He's roughed up— he fought me when I tried to take him from here. But he ain't dead. Yet," he added menacingly. "Why are you here? How did you know where to find me?"

"I didn't," she replied. "I was hoping you might come back here. It's where we met, remember?"

He blinked. "Yeah."

She put the leather pouch and the bags on the table. She opened the bag and produced two freshly buttered biscuits with strawberry preserves on them, along with a thermos of hot coffee. She presented them to him.

"Mavie's biscuits." His voice almost broke. He took one and bit into it and groaned with pleasure. He sipped coffee with the same expression. "Living in the wild, you miss some things so bad!" he exclaimed. He looked at her and winced. "Dangerous, you coming out here! Why did they let you?"

"They couldn't stop me," she said simply. She looked him in the eye. "I love Mallory Kirk."

That made him uncomfortable. He averted his eyes. "He ain't nothing to look at."

"It's what's inside him that makes him the man he is," she replied. "He's honest and hardworking and he never lies."

He laughed coldly. "That Bruner woman said she loved me," he said coldly. "I met her after my wife died. She wanted me to make her some keys. She said that man I killed owed her a ton of money and it was in his house in a box. She told him lies about his girl-friend to make him hit her. She knew the woman would call me for help, because I was close by."

"Good heavens," Morie exclaimed.

"So I got her out of the room and tried to make him tell me about the money in the box, but he fought me and I had to kill him. Gelly said it was all right . . . she had a way to make even more money," he said in a far-away tone. "She told me about the jeweled egg, but I already knew because Tank had showed it to me once. I didn't realize how much it was worth. So she took Mallory's keys and asked me to make her duplicates, to get into the Kirks' house and that curio cabi-net. She put them back and Mallory thought he'd misplaced them. I had to sneak into the smith's shop at night and risk capture to do it for her. She said she'd get that egg and sell it and then we'd have money to run away. She got a cowboy to help her. Then she goes and sells the stuff to a fence and gets arrested, and I don't get a dime, because Mallory Kirk called in a private detective and he blew the lid off the case!"

"My father called the detective," she said matter-of-factly. "I was blamed for the theft of the egg in the first place."

"You were?" he exclaimed.

She nodded. "By Gelly. And Bates, the cowboy who planted it in my bag."

"I hate that," he said slowly. "I never meant to hurt you. You been kind to me. Most people don't care."

"I'm sorry for you, I really am," she told him. "But killing Mallory won't solve any problems. It will just guarantee you the death penalty."

He laughed again, a cold, chilling sound, and his eyes were opaque. "I won't go back. I killed that man deliberately," he said, his eyes suddenly as cold as his voice. "He wouldn't tell me where the money was. I was going to have money to take Gelly places and buy her nice things. She said she loved me more than anybody in the world. Nobody loved me since my wife died. . . ."

Her heart stilled in her chest. She'd never known that Joe was involved with the woman. She would have bet that the Kirks didn't know, either.

"Did you know that she had a record?" she asked. "She was arrested twice and charged with theft, but she managed to get out of going to trial. She won't be that lucky this time."

"She said she had another way to get money, since this one fell through," he muttered. "She was going to claim that Mallory got her pregnant." He shook his head, while Morie stood frozen in place. "But after I kidnapped him, he told me he taped the conversation she had with him when she said it would be a lie but she could make people believe her. Can you believe she'd be that stupid?!"

Morie relaxed. She'd worried for a second that it could be true. It was such a relief! But she still had to save Mallory. . . .

"I brought you something else," she said, and indicated the leather pouch.

He frowned. He put down the thermos cup and opened the pouch. He caught his breath. "This is a fortune!"

"Not really. It's just five thousand. It's part of my inheritance. My father owns a big cattle ranch in Texas. His mother left me the money." She moved closer. "It will help you get away, won't it? So will you let Mallory go?"

His eyes narrowed suspiciously. "The bills are marked, huh?"

She threw up her hands. "How do you mark bills?" she exclaimed, exasperated. "I came straight from the bank to the airport, and I told nobody what I was going to do with the money. I didn't even tell my folks that I took it out of my account!"

He relaxed then. He took the money in his hands and looked at it with pure fascination. He'd done so many things, tried so hard, to get enough to get out of this county alive. Now he had the means. All he had to do was leave, now. . . .

"Were you followed?" he asked her at once.

She shook her head. "I made them promise."

He was thinking, planning, plotting. The money would buy him a cheap car, and clothes and food. He could run to Montana, where he had other friends who would hide him. He could get away.

He turned back to her and picked up the shotgun. For an instant, her heart shivered as she wondered if he'd kill her now that she'd given him the cash.

"I won't hurt you," he said in an awkward way. "I just want to get away. I can't go back to jail. I can't be locked up." He stared at the money. "I hit my mother with a tire iron," he recalled in a faraway, shocked tone. "I never meant to hurt her. I never meant to hurt anybody. I get these rages. I go blind mad and I can't control it. I can't help myself." He closed his eyes. "Maybe I'd be better off dead, you know? I wouldn't hurt anybody else. Poor old Mallory . . . he was kind to me once, gave me a helping hand because Tank asked him to, after we got out of military service. Tank was my friend. I lied to him. I told him I was framed." He sighed. "I wasn't framed. I meant to kill the man. I've done terrible things. Things I never wanted to do." He looked at her. "But I can't let them take me alive, you understand? I can't be locked up."

She grimaced. "If you gave yourself up, maybe they could get a psychologist who could help you. . . ."

"I killed a man," he reminded her. "And kidnapped another one. That means feds will come in. They'll track me all the way to hell. I can get away for a while. But in the end, the feds will hunt me down. I knew one, once. He was like a bulldog. Wouldn't eat, wouldn't sleep, just hunted until he found the man he was looking for. A lot of them are like that." He took the other biscuit and the thermos of coffee. "Thanks," he said. "For the food and coffee. For the money." He hesitated.

"For listening. Nobody ever really listened to me except my wife. I beat
her. . . ." He groaned. "God knows why
she didn't leave me. I never deserved
her. She got cancer. They said she
knew she had it and she wouldn't get
treatment. I knew why. She loved me
but she couldn't go on living with me,
and she couldn't leave me. Damn me! I
don't deserve to live!"

"That's not for you to say," she told
him. "Life is a gift."

He swallowed, hard. He looked at
her with eyes that were already dead.
"My mama knew there was something
wrong with me when I was little. She
said so. But she had too much pride to
tell anybody. Thought it was like saying
there was something wrong with her. I
could never learn nothing, you know? I
quit school because they made fun of
me. I saw words backward."

She went closer, totally unafraid. "I'm
sorry. I'm so sorry."

He ground his teeth together. "I'm
sorry I got you involved in this. Wasn't
your problem. Mallory's a half mile
down the trail," he said after a minute,

"off to the right, in some bushes. He'll be hard to find, because I didn't want him found."

"I'll find him," she said with certainty.

He started to the door, hesitated, looked back at her. "Damn, he's a lucky man!" he said through his teeth. He closed the door and melted into the night.

Morie didn't waste a minute. She rushed out, mounted the horse and turned him down the narrow trail that she knew from weeks of riding fence. Mallory was out there somewhere, getting soaked in this cold rain. God knew how long he'd been tied up. He would certainly need some sort of medical attention. It was almost freezing, unseasonably cold. She felt her heartbeat shaking her as she worried about not being able to find him. She could call for help, but if Joe was still around and watching, he might think she'd sold him out and he might try to kill Mallory and her in revenge. She didn't dare take the risk.

She rode down the path for what she

judged was a half mile, and she dismounted, tied her horse to a tree and started beating through the underbrush. But she found nothing. What if Joe had lied? What if he'd really killed Mallory, and she was going to stumble over his body instead of the living, breathing man? She felt terror rise in her throat like bile.

Maybe she'd misjudged the distance. Maybe it was farther away!

She mounted again and rode a little ways. Somewhere there was a sound, an odd sound, like a crack of thunder. But it was just drizzle. There was no storm. She shrugged it off. She was upset and hearing things. She dismounted and started searching off the path again. It was slow going. She could hardly see her hand in front of her face, and the flashlight was acting funny. She searched again and again, but she found nothing. There were trees, all around, but none with a man tied to it.

"Damn," she muttered, frantic to find Mallory. What if Bascomb had lied? What if he'd killed Mallory and dumped his body someplace else? If a man could kill, couldn't he lie, too?

She swallowed, hard, and fought tears. She had to think positively. Joe wasn't lying. Mallory was alive. He was somewhere around here. And she was going to find him! She had to find him. She had no life left without him.

She rode a few more yards, dismounted and searched off the path again. But, again, she found nothing. She repeated the exercise, over and over again, fearful that she might get careless and miss him. She could get help when it turned light, but that might be too late . . . !

She went down the path to a turn in the road, dismounted and walked through the underbrush. The glow of the flashlight began to give off a dull yellow light. She'd forgotten to change the batteries! She shook it and hit it, hoping the impact might prop it up for a few more precious minutes, but it didn't. Even as she watched, the light began to fade.

"Oh, damn!" she wailed to herself.

"And I haven't got any spare batteries. Of all the stupid things to do!"

There was a sound. She stopped. She listened. Rain was getting louder on the leaves, but there was some muffled sound. Her heart soared.

"Mallory!" she called. Damn Joe, she wasn't going to let Mal die because she was afraid to raise her voice.

The muffled sound came again, louder, to her right.

She broke through the bushes wildly, blindly, not caring if they tore her skin, if they ruined her clothing, if they broke bones. She trampled over dead limbs, through patchy weeds, toward a thicket where tall pine trees were growing.

"Mallory!" she called again.

"Here." His voice was muffled and bone-tired and heavy.

She pushed away some brush that had been piled up around a tree. And there was Mallory. Bareheaded, pale, tied to the tree with his arms behind him, sitting. He was soaking wet. His face was bruised. He looked worn to the bone. But when he saw Morie, his eyes were so brilliant with feeling that she caught her breath.

She managed to untie the bandanna that Joe had used to gag him with.

He coughed. "Got anything to drink?" he asked huskily. "Haven't had water for a day and a half. . . ."

"No," she groaned. "I'm so sorry!" She thought with anguish of the thermos of coffee she'd given Joe Bascomb.

"I'll get you loose," she choked out. She got around the tree and tried to untie the bonds, but the nylon rope was wet and it wouldn't budge.

"Pocketknife. Left pocket."

She dug in his pocket for it, her face close to his as she worked.

His dry mouth brushed across her cheek. "Beautiful, brave girl," he whispered. "So . . . proud of you."

Tears ran down her cheeks with the rain. She bent and put her mouth against his, hard. "I love you," she whispered. "I don't care about the past."

He managed a smile. "I love you, too, baby."

Her heart soared. "You do?" she exclaimed. "Oh, Mal!" She bent and kissed him again with helpless longing.

"I'm not complaining. But think you might cut me loose anytime soon?" he murmured. "My hands have gone to sleep."

"Oh, dear!"

She ran around the tree, opened the knife and went to work on the bonds. His hands were white. The circulation ran back into them when he was free and he groaned at the pain.

"Can you stand up?" she asked, concerned.

He tried and slumped back down. "Sorry," he murmured. "Legs gone to sleep, too."

He was obviously suffering from exposure and God knows what other sort of injuries that Joe had inflicted on him.

"I'll get help," she said at once, and pulled out her cell phone.

Lights flashed around her as men came forward. "Miss Brannt?" someone called.

She gasped. "Yes!"

A tall, dark-haired man came into view. He was wearing jeans and a buckskin jacket. He had long black hair in a ponytail and a grim expression. "I'm Ty Harding. I work for Dane Lassiter."

"Hiya, Harding," Mallory managed. "Good to see you on the job."

"I can outtrack any of these feds," he teased the other two men, "so I volunteered to help search for you. Hey, Jameson, can you bring a Jeep up here?"

"Sure. Be right back."

There were running footsteps.

Harding knelt beside him. "I don't think you're going to be able to ride a horse back," he guessed.

"Probably not," Mallory agreed hoarsely. "Have you got any water?"

"I have," one of the feds said, and tossed a bottle to Harding, who handed it, opened, to Mallory. It was painful to Morie to watch how thirstily he drank it, choked and drank again.

"God, that's so sweet!" Mallory exclaimed when he'd drained the bottle. "I've been tied here for almost two days. Thought I'd die, sure. Then an angel came walking up and saved me," he added, smiling at Morie. "My own personal guardian angel."

"I gave Joe Bascomb a pouch with cash," she told Harding. "I spoke to the sheriff about it before I came up here, so he knows. I can't tell you which direction Joe took. It was raining. . . ."

Harding's expression in the light of his flashlight was grim. "There's no need to concern yourself with that now."

"Have you caught him?" she exclaimed. "Already?"

"No," he said quietly. "We found him. Sitting up against a tree about half a mile away. Stone dead."

She caught her breath. Cold chills ran up and down her arms. That odd, high-pitched crack of thunder she thought she'd heard. A gunshot? "Dead?" She faltered.

He nodded. "Self-inflicted gunshot wound. He left a note." He pulled it out of his pocket. "He addressed it to you, Miss Brannt."

With trembling hands, she opened the dirty piece of paper. It was stained with blood. Joe's blood. It was only a few lines of scribbled writing.

I killed a man and kidnapped another on account of a no-good woman who just wanted money. I'd never get out of jail. Thank you for being kind, when nobody else ever was. Your man is lucky. Be happy. Your friend, Joe.

She burst into tears.

Mallory pulled her close and held her, despite the pain in his arms from being in such a restrained position. "It's all right. It's all over."

"Poor man," she choked out.

"He chose his life, Miss Brannt," Harding told her quietly.

"But he didn't," she said through tears. "He had a learning disability and all sorts of psychological problems. But he didn't get help because his mother thought they'd say there was something wrong with her, too."

"Good Lord," Mallory said heavily. "If only we'd known."

"We all have a purpose," Morie said again.

"Yes, we do," Harding said, surprisingly. "People weave themselves into the fabric of our lives for reasons we sometimes never understand. But there is a purpose to everything. Even Bascomb's suicide."

"At least his mother didn't live to see him come to this end," Mallory said. He tilted up Morie's wet face. "And speaking of family, we'd better start making telephone calls. My brothers must be out of their minds, to say nothing of your mother and brother and your vicious, rabid father. . . ."

"He isn't vicious. You'll learn to love him," she assured him.

"Think so?" Harding mused, pursing his lips. "I've met your father. And I have serious doubts about that."

She chuckled. "You don't know him. I do."

"My loss, I'm sure," Harding conceded. He looked up as the Jeep arrived. "Let's get you to the hospital, Mr. Kirk. You'll need to be checked out."

"Hospital? I'm not going to any

damned hospital!" he burst out as they helped him into the Jeep.

"Yes, you are," Morie told him firmly. "Now sit back and shut up. We're saving you."

He gave her a blank stare. And then he chuckled. "Okay, boss," he drawled. "Whatever you say."

"You just remember that, and we'll get along famously." She batted her long lashes at him and grinned.

CHAPTER THIRTEEN

Tank and Cane met them at the emergency room. They hugged their pale, worn brother and choked up at the thought of how close he'd come to death.

"You let her come out after me alone," Mallory accused them.

"You can thrash us when you're better. Honest, we'll break you a pine limb," Cane promised.

Tank grinned. "But look what she did. She saved you."

Morie beamed. "Yes, I did," she agreed. "Despite the best efforts of my brother and mother and father and your brothers and Darby."

"We're all relieved," Cane said, smiling at her. "But she did what none of us could have done. Bascomb would have shot us on sight. . . ."

There was a commotion in the hall followed by angry footsteps and a loud voice.

"Dad!" Morie exclaimed, because she recognized that voice.

King Brannt stormed into the examination room with flashing black eyes, trailed by a hospital clerk and a resident.

"Oh, Dad!" Morie ran and hugged him close. "I'm okay. It's all right!"

"Where is he?" They could hear Shelby's voice in the hall.

"Just follow the trail of bodies," Cort answered with a laugh.

"Mom! Cort! What are you doing here?" she exclaimed, hugging them, too.

"We were ten minutes behind you," King said, "but we couldn't get anybody to tell us anything, and they—" he pointed at Cane and Tank "—wouldn't answer their damned phones. I had to yell at a detective and a sheriff to find out anything!"

"You shouldn't yell at people. It's undignified," Shelby said gently.

He glared at her. "It's justified when you're scared to death that your daughter's been killed!"

The resident and the hospital clerk belatedly understood King's rampage. They smiled and left. The resident was back in a minute, however, to check out Mallory.

"Exposure, dehydration, some evidence of bruising on the ribs and a dislocated shoulder, but the tests don't reveal any broken bones or internal injuries," he told them. "You were very lucky, Mr. Kirk. Far luckier than your assailant. They've just taken him to the local hospital for an autopsy."

"What?" King exclaimed.

"Killed himself," the resident explained. He looked at Morie and shook his head. "If my wife had done what you did tonight, I'd have eaten her alive verbally before I hugged her to death.

Does foolhardy behavior run in your family?"

"Yes, it does!" Shelby volunteered, pointing toward her husband and her son.

"Well, Mr. Kirk will be all right," the resident said with a smile. "He just needs rest and something for pain and a little patching up. We'll take care of that right now."

"Patching up," Mallory muttered. "It's just some cuts. I get worse than this doing ranch work every day."

"Me, too," King agreed, approaching him with his hands in his pockets. "Got kicked by a bull two days ago and had to have stitches."

"I got stepped on by one last week," Mallory said. "Damned things do it deliberately."

King stared at him. "You'd better be good to her."

"I will," Mallory replied quietly.

"You bet he will," Tank seconded. "Or we'll make him divorce her and I'll marry her and be good to her."

"She can marry me if she decides to get rid of him." Cane jerked his thumb toward Mallory. "I still have most of my own teeth and I can do the tango," he claimed with a straight face, because he'd heard from Mallory about Morie's fascination with the dance.

"I'm learning," Mallory protested. "It takes time. I need somebody to teach me."

Morie pursed her lips. "I think I'm up to that."

Mallory's dark eyes twinkled. "I think I'll learn even faster if you teach me. And there are a few things I can teach you, too."

"There are?" she asked, with mock fascination.

"Yes. Like how not to go riding off into the dark looking for escaped con-victs!" he burst out. "What if he'd killed you?"

"Then I guess you'd have to find somebody else to teach you how to tango," she said simply.

Mallory let out an exasperated sigh.

"See?" King asked him. "Now you know how it's going to be. I've put up with it since she was old enough to stamp her foot at me and say no. It's your turn now."

Morie just laughed.

She didn't go home with her family. She moved into the big house at the Kirk ranch, into her own room, and Mallory bought her a beautiful set of rings, but emeralds instead of rubies. He wasn't duplicating the Fortune 500 heir's offering, he assured her. They were engaged although he'd never actually asked her to marry him. Shelby was helping with invitations. The ceremony would be held at the ranch in Texas.

The night before they flew back, Mallory held her in his lap in the recliner in the living room, after his brothers had discreetly gone to bed. He kissed her hungrily.

"I'm starving," he groaned as his hands found their way under her flimsy blouse and molded the soft skin. "I've never been so hungry in all my life."

She smiled under the warm press of his mouth. "Me, either."

"But we're going to wait anyway."

She laughed. "Yes."

He lifted his head. He was breathing hard. "Remind me again why we're going to do that, when nobody else does?"

"Just because the whole world's doing it, doesn't make it right in the view of people of faith," she replied simply. "I want a wedding night. A real one. Not an after-the-fact one that just comes after the wedding ceremony. I want oceans of lace in the gown I choose, the excitement of the ceremony and the reception, and the anticipation of how wonderful it's going to be during the night ahead. There's only one first time. Mine is going to be exactly the way I want it. Period."

He sighed. "Principles are very cumbersome sometimes."

She leaned forward and nibbled his lower lip. "You'll be happy you waited."

"Are you sure about that?" he mused.

She nodded. "Positively."

"All right. I'll have a cold shower and a colder beer and go to bed."

"Good man."

He made a face. "Not willingly."

"You're a good man," she disagreed. "And I'll be very proud to be your wife."

He smiled. "My beautiful Morena," he whispered. "Married to the ugliest tough man in Wyoming."

"Liar," she chided. "You're the most gorgeous man alive to me."

His eyebrows arched. "Me?"

"You. It isn't the way you look that makes you gorgeous. It's the man you are."

He flushed.

She grinned. She kissed him again and got to her feet. "We leave first thing in the morning. Mavie and Darby have to come, too, you know."

"They know, too. They're packed already."

She was somber for a moment. "I'm really sorry about Gelly. They say she'll probably do twenty years if they convict her."

"I'm sorry I blamed you," he replied, hugging her close. He sighed. "I had a close call there. She really had me with blinders on."

"You woke up in time, though. That's what counts."

"I suppose it does."

*　*　*

The wedding was the biggest event Branntville could remember since Shelby Kane married King Brannt. The guest list was incredible. It included famous movie stars and television newsmen, sports stars, politicians and even European royalty.

Daryl was on the guest list. He had come by earlier to congratulate them, and to tell Morena he was happy for her. He hadn't been offended that Morena sent the rings back instead of returning them herself, especially when he knew what she'd risked to save Mallory's life. He was just happy that she was safe.

However, he added ruefully, now that he was no longer engaged, his enthusiastic parents were once again offering him as an entrée to any eligible young woman. He was resigned, he told her, to being hunted. But who knew, they might find him someone really nice. Like his friend Morena. Mallory stood by, not very patiently, while they spoke. But Daryl shook hands with him and after a few minutes, they were all smiling.

As they settled into the wedding ceremony, Morena, in a designer gown that one of Shelby's former colleagues had made up for her, was radiant and so much in love that she seemed to glow. Her black hair, festooned with pale white pearl flowers, was loose around her shoulders under a veil of illusion with pearl highlights that covered her face. Her gown was traditional, with puff sleeves and a keyhole neckline, a long train . . . and it was accented with imported Belgian lace. Her jewelry was some of the finer pieces from her mother's collection along with a borrowed jeweled hair clasp from her shy maid of honor, Odalie Everett, who walked down the aisle tall and proud on the arm of Cane Kirk to stand with Mallory, pointedly ignoring Cort Brannt along the way.

The organ sounded the "Wedding March" as Morena walked slowly down the aisle of the ranch chapel to Mallory Kirk, who was standing at the altar with both his brothers as best man. She carried a bouquet of white and yellow roses tied with yellow ribbon. She looked at Mallory and almost tripped at the expression in his dark, loving eyes. *What a long way we've come,* she thought.

She looked up at him and the rest of the ceremony went by so quickly that she almost missed it. She let him put the ring on her finger, said the appropriate words and peered up at her new husband as he lifted the fingertip veil from her face and saw her for the first time as a wife. It was an old, beautiful tradition that both had looked forward to, in a time when tradition was routinely trampled and ridiculed by the world at large.

"My beautiful wife," he whispered, and smiled as he bent to kiss her with tender reverence.

She kissed him back, sighing as if she had the world in her arms. And she did.

The reception was fun. They fed each other cake, posed for pictures for the press and the photographer who was documenting the wedding, and danced to the live orchestra playing contemporary tunes.

"What a long way we've come," Mallory murmured into her ear as he waltzed her around the room.

"Funny, I was thinking that when we were standing at the altar," she exclaimed.

"Reading each other's minds already," he teased.

She nodded. Her eyes searched his. The electricity between them arced like a live current. She caught her breath at the intensity of feeling there.

"Not yet," she whispered.

He nodded, but his eyes never left hers. "Not yet."

Two long hours later, they climbed into the limousine that was taking them to San Antonio, where they were spending their wedding night. The next day, they were off to the Caribbean, to a private island owned by a friend who was loaning them his estate for a week. It would be a dream honeymoon. Nothing to do but learn about each other and lie in the sun. Morena was looking forward to it.

They checked in to the suite Mallory

had reserved. The bellboy was tipped. The door was locked. The phone was unplugged. Mallory took Morena by the waist and looked into her eyes for so long that she gasped with the feeling that passed between them.

He reached out with a long forefinger and traced a path around a nipple which quickly became erect. She gasped.

"I've dreamed about this for weeks," he whispered.

She nodded, breathless. "So have I."

He bent and nuzzled his nose against hers. The pressure of his finger increased, teasing and withdrawing. "You made me wait," he whispered with patient amusement. "Now I'm going to make you wait."

His mouth opened on hers. He kissed her slowly, with a mastery she was only just beginning to recognize. His big hands were deft and sure as he peeled her out of the exquisite dress and the slip and bra underneath. He kissed his way down her trembling body to her panty line as he eased the last flimsy scraps of clothing from her. His mouth opened on her flat belly and she cried out as his hands moved lower.

He let her go long enough to turn down the bedcovers. He lifted her, kissed her tenderly and laid her on the cool sheets. His eyes made a meal of her nudity as his hands went to his coat. He removed it, and then the tie. He dropped them onto a chair and smiled as his hands worked buttons on his shirt to disclose a broad, muscular chest covered with thick, curling black hair.

She thought about how that was going to feel against her bare breasts and she moved, helpless, on the sheets, shivering a little at the intensity of his gaze.

He chuckled softly. "Anticipation is fun," he murmured.

"Says you," she teased, breathless.

He removed his shoes and socks, his belt, his trousers. Then, slowly, the black boxer shorts he fancied.

She stared at him with red cheeks. She'd seen photographs. Most women had, at some point, even if it was only by looking over a classmate's shoulder at a magazine. But she hadn't dreamed that men looked so, so . . .

As she looked, he began to swell from the pleasure of her rapt gaze, and she did gasp.

He eased down beside her on the bed. "As you might have guessed," he whispered in a voice gone husky with desire, "I'm a little better endowed than most men. But I won't hurt you. I promise."

"I'm not afraid."

"Bosh." His mouth smoothed over her firm, pretty little breasts. "Of course you are. It's the first time."

"Of course I am," she agreed huskily. "You don't mind . . . ?"

He lifted his head and looked at her with open shock. "What?"

"I read this article," she said. "Some men said they wouldn't touch a virgin because they didn't want to have to worry about complications . . ."

"They did?" His hand slid down her belly and he smiled as she tried to withdraw when he touched her. "Easy," he whispered. "This is part of it. Don't be embarrassed. It's natural, what you're feeling."

She didn't know what she was feeling. Shock, at first, at being touched in a place where she only touched herself when she was bathing. And then, more shock, because when his hand moved, there was so much pleasure that she cried out and clutched at his arms.

"Unexpected, was it?" he teased gently. "Oh, it gets better."

His mouth opened on her soft breasts while he touched her, tasting and exploring in a veritable feast of the senses that lifted her in a helpless arch toward the source of all that delight.

"This may be a little uncomfortable," he whispered at her mouth as his hand moved again.

She flinched at first. But when she realized what he was doing, she didn't fight. She lay back, biting her lower lip, until he finished.

When he lifted his hand, there was a trace of blood. He reached beside the bed for a box of tissues and wiped it off, looking into her eyes the whole time.

"It wasn't bad," she whispered.

He nodded. "It will hurt less, now, when I go inside you," he whispered, moving down against her. He nudged her legs apart matter-of-factly, looking down. "I'll go slow."

"Okay."

She lifted her arms to him and welcomed the warm, slow crush of his chest against her breasts. She gasped as she felt him at the secret place, the dark place that had never known contact such as this. Her nails bit into his hard arms as he nudged at her gently.

He reassured her. "Nothing to be nervous about," he said softly. "Nothing at all."

His hand moved in between their bodies and touched her. This time she didn't flinch. She lifted up to it and shivered as pleasure throbbed into her like molten fire. She moaned and closed her eyes, so that she could savor it.

The pressure grew little by little, tracing and teasing, and then firm, and insistent, and maddening.

"Please!" she cried.

"Yes."

His hand moved and his body re-placed it. He moved into her deliber-ately, confidently, resting on his fore-arm as he positioned her for even greater pleasure and guided her move-ments.

She sobbed. The tension was grow-ing, building. She couldn't think. She could barely breathe. She focused on his face, coming closer, moving away, on the rhythm that brushed her against the mattress with every slow, deep thrust of his hips. She shivered as the pleasure kept building and building and building, breath by aching breath, until the whole world reduced itself to the sound of their bodies sliding against each other, the faint scraping sound of the sheets as they moved over them, the building rasp of their breathing.

"Mallory," she sobbed, arching, shud-dering.

"Now, baby," he whispered, and the rhythm increased and his body became demanding, as control slipped away. "Now, now, now!"

She cried out, clutching him as she moved, too, desperate to twist up and meet that hard thrust, make it deeper, make it harder, make it, make it, make it . . . blaze up . . . like a furnace!

Her teeth bit into him as she climaxed, her body convulsing in a tense arch as she drowned in pleasure she'd never dreamed could exist. She was barely aware of his own rough movement, the hoarse cries of pleasure at her ears as he went over the edge with her. They clung together in ecstasy, as passion spent itself over a space of heated, mad seconds.

And even then, they couldn't stop moving. She ground her hips up against his, pleading for more.

"Oh, don't stop," she pleaded.

"I can't," he whispered in a hoarse chuckle. "Sweet. So damned sweet. I thought I was going to die of it!"

"Me, too!"

He lifted his head as he moved down against her, watching her pleasure grow all over again. Her response delighted him, made him feel ten feet tall. She showed no sign of wanting to stop at all.

"Go ahead, gloat," she whispered unsteadily.

"I love you," he whispered back, and kissed her hungrily. "My brave, beautiful, unbelievably sexy wife. I'd die for you."

She hugged him close. "I'd die for you."

His mouth crushed down over hers. "I'm spent, baby," he whispered against her lips. "But I can last a little longer. I'll pleasure you as long as I can, okay?"

She wasn't hearing him, or understanding him. She was in the grip of a fever so hot she thought she would burn to death. But finally, finally, she shuddered one last time and the tension snapped. She collapsed under him with a trembling sigh.

He rolled over beside her and gathered her close. "Satisfied?"

"Yes. I don't understand," she whispered into his throat.

"Women take longer than men do," he explained. "But a man spends himself and it takes time for him to be able to go again. Women last a lot longer in passion."

"Oh."

He lifted his head and searched her eyes. "You were right."

"I was? About what?"

He kissed her eyelids. "About waiting." He looked at her solemnly. "Right now, I'm sorry that I ever had a woman in my life before I met you."

She touched his mouth gently. "I'm not sure I'm sorry," she whispered drily.

He lifted both eyebrows.

"You are very, very good in bed," she mused. "From a beginner's standpoint, I mean. I was afraid," she confessed. "I'd heard some horror stories from other women about wedding nights. Especially about men losing control and hurting them badly."

"Oh, I couldn't hurt you," he replied softly and kissed her again. "I love you too much. It had to be good for you, or it wouldn't have been good for me at all."

She smiled lazily and moved against him, but suddenly she winced.

He lifted an eyebrow. "Sore?"

She flushed.

He laughed indulgently. "It's a side

effect of headlong passion and absti-
nence. Not to worry, a couple of days'
rest and we'll be back to normal. Meanwhile," he added with a chuckle, "we
might consider ordering food and
watching something on pay-per-view.
What do you say?"

She sat up, gingerly, and nodded.
"That might be a good idea."

He stood up, stretched and then
grinned at her admiring gaze, picked
her up and carried her into the bath-
room. "But first we can have a nice re-
laxing shower and play doctor!"

She burst out laughing. Not only was
marriage a passion feast, it also seemed
to be the most fun she'd ever had.

A week later, they were doing the tango
in an exclusive club in Jamaica, right
on the beach.

"I told you I'd learn quickly with the
right teacher," Mallory teased, kissing
her ear as they moved around the room.

"Yes, and you did."

"So did you," he whispered outrageously.

She peered up at him mischievously. "I bought this book today."

"You did? A book?" He leaned down. "What sort of book?"

"It's a detailed book about how to, well, how to do stuff. With your husband."

"I don't have a husband," he groaned. "What about me?"

"It's a book for a woman about how to do stuff with her husband," she informed him. "It's very detailed."

"Does it have pictures?" he asked with wide eyes.

She glared at him. "It doesn't need pictures."

"Then, can you demonstrate it for me?" he added, and his dark eyes were twinkling.

She laughed out loud. "Oh, I think I can do that."

"Now?" he asked, stopping in the middle of the dance floor.

"Here?" she asked, horrified.

"How dare you?" he huffed. "I'm a decent, upright man, I am."

"You can't be upright while I demonstrate this book," she pointed out. She pursed her lips. "You have to be in a reclining position."

"This is getting better by the minute. Shall we go?"

He held out his arm. She put hers through it with a chuckle. "By all means. It might take some time," she added as they left the room. "I'm not sure I've got it down pat just yet."

"I promise not to complain, no matter how long it takes," he assured her with laughing dark eyes.

It did take a very long time. But he kept his promise. He didn't complain. Not even once.

* * * * *